WORKING GIRL
'Fractured'
Book One

By ROXY
RICH

WORKING GIRL
'Fractured'
Book One
Roxy Rich

WORKING GIRL 'Fractured' Book one.

Copyright @ 2024 Roxy Rich.

All rights reserved. No part of this publication may be reproduced, distributed, or transmitted in any form or by any means, including photocopying, recording, or other electronic or mechanical methods, without the prior written permission of the author.

Legal Disclaimer.

This is a work of fiction. Unless otherwise indicated, all the names, characters, businesses, places, events and incidents in this book are either the product of the author's imagination or used in a fictitious manner. Any resemblance to actual persons, living or dead, or actual events are purely coincidental.

WARNING.

This book entails, human trafficking, child prostitution, prostitution, domestic abuse, drug addiction and murder. Along with scenes of rape and torture. Please do not read if you have a delicate constitution.

Table of Contents

Title Page 1
Copyright Page 2
Dedications 7
CHAPTER 1: Ripped apart. 8
CHAPTER 2: Trophies and atrocities 14
CHAPTER 3: Why didn't you die? 20
CHAPTER 4: Time to heal. 24
CHAPTER 5: The Devils at the door. 31
CHAPTER 6: Always watching. 37
CHAPTER 7: Mechanism of Control. 42
CHAPTER 8: Requisition. 48
CHAPTER 9: Emptiness. 52
CHAPTER 10: New blood. 57
CHAPTER 11: Grieving. 61
CHAPTER 12: City lights. 66
CHAPTER 13: Inflicted wounds. 72
CHAPTER 14: Torture. 77
CHAPTER 15 Inevitable. 82
CHAPTER 16: The Doctor 88
CHAPTER 17: Creep. 96
CHAPTER 18: Home truths. 100
CHAPTER 19: Evil. 103
CHAPTER 20: Broken wings. 108
CHAPTER 21: The detective 113
CHAPTER 22: Vengeance is mine. 117
CHAPTER 23: Deadly encounters. 123
CHAPTER 24: The birthday. 126
CHAPTER 25: Violation. 130
CHAPTER 26: Gone. 133
CHAPTER 27: No allies. 138
CHAPTER 28: Destroyer. 142
CHAPTER 29: Help us. 145
CHAPTER 30: Forgive me. 149
CHAPTER 31: A rude awakening. 154
CHAPTER 32: Bloodied and battered. 158

CHAPTER 33: Mercy. 161
CHAPTER 34: Left alone. 166
CHAPTER 35: The carparks. 170
CHAPTER 36: Unspeakable. 175
CHAPTER 37: Frozen. 179
CHAPTER 38: The price of freedom. 183
Sign up for Roxy Rich's Mailing List 188
Further Reading: WORKING GIRL 'Afflicted' 189

Dedications

For my wonderful friends Fiona Barry and Deb Page, who have both kept me going through the good times and the bad.

To my amazing husband who always believed in me, when no one else ever did. You've stood by me through thick and thin, through loss and grief. You are my soulmate, my best friend and my world.

Lastly, I would like to thank my proofreader, Jill Goss. Jillgoss87@gmail.com

CHAPTER 1: Ripped apart.

'Memories'

'It was a day I will always remember, the day it happened. I was awakened by the sound of the bathroom faucet running. I could see the floor was wet, soaking the carpet in the hallway, as I drew nearer. I still get a sick feeling in my stomach when I think about it. I looked down at my feet, which were engulfed in puddles and the ripples of the icy water were turning my feet blue. The coldness made me shudder as I reached for the bathroom doorknob. My world fell apart, when I saw my mother in the bathtub, with a needle sticking out of her flesh with a plastic tube looped around her arm. Her skin had shrivelled up from the icy bath water, and although her eyes were open, she was not responding. I tried to wake her up by shaking her, but it was too late. I screamed, but nothing came out. My mother had died. According to the paramedics, my mother had been lying there dead for several hours. I remember screaming at my sister to stay away from the bathroom and to get some towels, while I was having trouble turning off the taps. Before I knew it, I was scrubbing the floor, trying to mop up the mess, whilst my heart was shattering. There was nothing else I could do, I felt so useless. I am thankful that I, and not my sister Alice, found our mother, even though I hate that this day will always be etched in my memory. It hurts so much. Sadly, it's the last thing I will ever remember about her. Right now, all I can think of is her lifeless body in that bathtub. I've forgotten the warmth of her embraces, the smell of her skin, and the sound of her laughter. Every time I close my eyes, I see my mother dead in the bath. Why did she do it? Why? I suppose I'll have to wait to find out when I go to heaven. One day, I hope, I will be able to hug her once more, see her face, and experience the warmth of her embrace. Other times, I just feel terrible for being so angry at her. Why did she leave us behind?'

SHE WAS A LOST AND empty soul, her life had been incredibly difficult. At the tender age of twelve, Jolene lost her mother to a drug overdose. Her stepfather, a Yardie, was a cruel and mean man. Her ten year old sister was her only source of solace, she knew she had to protect her, despite being just a child herself. On the day of the funeral, their stepfather made them clean the house for his friends. None of her mother's friends or family would attend, as those connections had long been severed. Sitting in the kitchen Jolene brushed and braided her sister's long hair. The two sisters resembled delicate porcelain dolls, with their piercing blue eyes, fair skin, and silky platinum blonde hair. Jolene sensed that her life was now over, her only shield had departed this world. She would become the protector, assuming the role of both mother and guardian. Her world had become confined and suffocating. Since her mother's departure, she was no longer allowed to attend school. Her stepfather made sure she stayed at home with him, taking over the responsibilities her mother had once shouldered. For now, her sister was still allowed to go to school. Jolene despised how her stepfather watched their every move, monitoring her daily chores and reprimanding her if the house wasn't impeccably clean or if his dinner wasn't served precisely at six o'clock every evening. Despite her recent loss, he had already subjected her to several beatings, simply because the dinner wasn't ready on time. She felt trapped, she had even reached out to social services for help, pleading for them to place them in care and spare them from her stepfather's clutches. The social worker who came seemed uninterested, and oddly friendly with her stepfather, allowing him to retain custody and guardianship over the sisters. Jolene couldn't fathom why. Her stepfather had a notorious reputation, known to the authorities as a drug dealer and pimp, and this terrified her the most. He seemed to possess an inexplicable power over everyone in his circle, including the police, local thugs, and even the neighbours, who revered him. It appeared that he was untouchable. Her poor mother had been reduced to a helpless addict by him, forced to work on the streets. Jolene would never forgive him for that. She felt like he had murdered her mother. Prior to meeting him, they struggled financially, but Jolene's mother always did her best with what they had, ensuring the girls were clean and fed. After her mother and Otis were married, Jolene's world had been turned upside down, and her mother was forever changed, she became a mere shadow of her former self. Money and drugs were her sole focus, and not in that order. Jolene's life was far from normal, but her mother still attempted to make her and her sister as comfortable as possible. Despite everything, her mother still loved them above all else. On the day of the funeral, her stepfather's best friend arrived to collect them.

    The funeral would take place at the local crematorium and would be a relatively modest event. Jolene's sister Alice couldn't stop crying. Their stepfather demanded that she quiet down, but she couldn't be consoled. Jolene tried everything to calm her sister, but to no avail. Then their driver, her stepfather's best friend, handed Jolene two tablets and said, "Here, take these. They will help calm both of you." Jolene didn't know what the tablets were, but she weakly smiled at the man and her stepfather, and reluctantly took them. She gave one to her sister and swallowed one herself. She presumed they were Valium or diazepam from her mother's stash. Jolene didn't want to take the drugs after witnessing her mother's fate, but she knew that if she didn't calm her sister down, she would face further punishment later. She didn't want to bear any more pain on this day. Today was meant to be a day of remembrance for her mother and the love she had shown them. Both girls would deeply miss her. Little did they know that their lives were about to take a horrifying turn, they were completely unaware of the imminent danger ahead.

    The funeral was a solemn affair, attended only by a few of Otis's women, his best friend Shady, the girls themselves, and their stepfather. The tablets they had taken kept the girls quiet and subdued throughout the service. No tears were shed as their mother's coffin was taken down to the incinerators. Afterward, they stood at the doors of the crematorium, allowing guests to offer their condolences. The women in attendance were all employees of their stepfather, dressed inappropriately in their sex work attire. One of them, Maria, had been a close friend of their mother. She gave the girls packets of sweets and assured them of her support. Maria, once a beautiful woman, had been ravaged by drug abuse and the hardships of street work. Although she had always been kind to the girls, Jolene secretly blamed her for her mother's downfall. It was Maria who had introduced their mother to Otis.

Jolene believed that their lives would have been completely different if not for Maria's involvement. Maria had jet black hair and a European appearance, with a slim frame and an extremely large bust. Despite everything, her hair remained long, black, and silky. Otis had a peculiar obsession with long hair, and all his women were required to have it. Jolene made a shocking discovery one day while putting away laundry in Otis's room. She found a collection of locks of hair, including her mother's hair neatly stored in a clear bag attached to a folder. Each bag was labelled and dated. Some bags had "DEAD YARN" written on them in bold letters, though she couldn't comprehend the meaning. Ever since her mum's death, Jolene would occasionally enter Otis's room under the guise of tidying up or making his bed, just to touch and smell her mother's hair. Otis would cut locks of hair from all his girls and keep them as trophies in his collection. This peculiar hobby had begun in his childhood, but his mother had discovered it and thrown away his collection. His strict evangelist mother had vehemently condemned his actions. After her death, Otis vowed to never let a woman control his life again. He saw no harm in collecting locks of hair from the unsuspecting women of Birmingham, believing his mother's reaction to be absurd. Little did Jolene know, Otis's dark nature extended far beyond the hair collection. He abused and exploited women as a way to seek revenge for his perceived past grievances. His deep-seated hatred for women originated from the sexual and physical abuse he endured from his own mother, who sold him as a child. She had moulded him into the monster he had become, viewing women as objects, to be used until they were no longer of use. He had understood from a young age that people were commodities.

Even though he was a pimp, he concealed a much darker secret, he kept trophies of his atrocities. He was intent on expanding into trafficking minors, seeing it as a lucrative endeavour. If he could coerce the girls into working for him, he hoped they would help recruit others. These twisted thoughts occupied Otis's mind, as he sought to perpetuate his cycle of violence and revenge.

Once his women hit the streets, they lost their allure for him. His true nature, shocking and devoid of empathy, would subdue the unsuspecting women. Sex was never his real desire; it didn't stir any genuine emotions within him. He used it as a means to gain their trust and affection. His bones lacked any trace of humanity, a result of his mother's abuse. He had learned a long time ago, to shut down any semblance of human connection, considering emotions nothing but a burden. With their mother now out of the picture, he saw an opportunity to exploit the sisters, just like he did to everyone else in his deviant world. It wouldn't take long for the young girls to start earning him money. He had a few high-paying clients lined up, eagerly waiting to take their innocence. Once he had brought the sisters home, his plan was to drug their drinks, leaving them unconscious for the wealthy men he had invited to deflower them. A steady stream of clients had been arranged, including the corpulent and sweaty social worker, who had a disturbing preference for young girls. Gathering such information wasn't difficult, word travelled among the younger girls on the strip, it was widely known, which social workers would trade sex for haircuts or new clothes. Although Otis despised the man, as he reminded him of his own abusers from childhood, he saw him as a means to an end. This night promised a lucrative pay out, and Otis was determined to ensure everything ran smoothly.

 As they sat in the back of the car, Jolene and Alice, sobbed quietly, finding comfort in each other's arms. They had just buried their mother, and their world had crumbled. Jolene's main concern was getting her sister home safely and tucking her into bed. Neither of them had an appetite, but Jolene still had to cook for her stepfather. Thoughts raced through her mind as the car sped through the streets of Birmingham, she worried about protecting her younger sister from the horrors that await them. Jolene, desperate to shield her sister, made a decision, she would do whatever Otis asked, as long as it kept her sister out of harm's way. She would take on her mother's responsibilities, even if it meant engaging in a relationship with Otis. Little did she know the sinister plans Otis had in store for both of them.

 On arriving home, Otis's unusually kind demeanour caught the girls off guard. He even went as far as making them hot chocolate, a rare gesture. Each sister received a chocolate bar, and Otis engaged them in pleasant conversation while they sat at the table. Grateful for his attention, they drank their hot chocolate, oblivious to the danger lurking within. Jolene's last memory was witnessing a stranger carrying her sister to the bedroom, a man she didn't recognise from Otis's circle of friends. Reality blurred into a hazy fog, and her body felt heavy as she slumped against the table. Meanwhile, Otis stationed himself outside the girls' bedroom, collecting payment from each man who entered to exploit the drugged bodies of the sisters. He aimed to ensure they were not excessively harmed, as he needed them back on their feet soon. He had arranged for each girl to be taken by five men, all of whom paid a substantial amount of money for the privilege.

This single night alone, would earn him more than what some of his other women made for him, in a week. Otis knew their value would diminish once their innocence was lost, leaving him with the challenge of maintaining their worth in his immoral business. Once they were broken in, they would earn for him. His true colours would shock the unsuspecting girls, as it had his other women, manipulating them into submission. With the older women that worked for him, sex was just an act, he would use it merely as a weapon to gain their trust and affection. That was his normal "modus operandi". Devoid of humanity, he had mastered the art, to suppress any human emotion long ago. These young girls would make him a fortune, especially now that their mother was out of the picture, there was no one left to protect them. He had ensured her demise with a fatal heroin injection. With her gone, he could exploit her daughters and pimp them to the highest bidders.

CHAPTER 2: Trophies and atrocities

As the sun began its ascent into the sky, casting a golden hue upon the world, Jolene emerged from the depths of her slumber. A restless night clung to her like a shroud, leaving her disoriented and dishevelled. Every fibre of her being throbbed with a dull ache, a testament to the physical toll exacted upon her. She stood there, perplexed, her brow furrowed in confusion. The world around her seemed to blur as she grappled with the scene before her. She could hear haunting whimpers, causing her to freeze in her tracks. With a sense of urgency, she hurried towards the source of the sound, her eyes scanning the room for any signs of distress.

As she drew closer, her gaze fell upon Alice, her delicate frame trembling with fear. A gasp escaped her lips, as she noticed the tell-tale marks of violence etched upon Alice's thighs. In that moment, a shocking realisation struck her like a bolt of lightning, sending shivers down her spine. Jolene and her sister had fallen victim to a nefarious plot. Their lives had taken a sinister turn as they were surreptitiously drugged, their senses dulled, and their wills weakened. Unbeknown to them, they had become the latest pawns in Otis's human trafficking ring. Their bedroom, once a sanctuary of safety, now exuded an air of desolation, the walls seemingly closing in on them like a foreboding prison.

In the wake of their mother's passing, Otis showed no mercy, denying them even a single day to mourn. Just as Jolene began to process the loss, a piercing cry escaped Alice's lips, her voice filled with anguish, as she uttered the haunting words, "Blood, blood." Jolene's keen eyes caught sight of the crimson stain seeping through Alice's nightdress. "Don't worry Alice," she said with a hint of reassurance. Her heart, once a bastion of hope and love, now shattered into a thousand jagged pieces. The weight of her sorrow pressed upon her frail frame, every inch of her being consumed by an unrelenting ache. Yet, it was her mind, once sharp and vibrant, that suffered the most. Like a delicate porcelain doll dropped from a great height, her thoughts lay scattered and fractured, unable to be pieced back together. The air hung heavy with betrayal. The question lingered in the minds of those present, how could Otis, their stepfather, commit such a heinous act against them? The room fell silent.

Both were previously innocent and untouched by the harsh realities of the world; they were mere children. Alice's tears cascaded down her face, each droplet a testament to her anguish. Jolene, desperately sought to soothe her trembling form, her gentle words a balm for Alice's shattered soul. The petite frame of her sister bore the tell-tale signs of a violent encounter, adorned with a tapestry of discoloured patches that marred her delicate skin. Jolene, with a heart full of vengeance, found herself unwilling to confront Otis at that moment. The burning desire to extinguish his life consumed her, yet she understood the insurmountable challenge that lay before her. Her heart raced as she cautiously approached the bathroom, her mind a single thought, would he be there?

The anticipation of an empty home, devoid of his presence, fuelled her hopes and desires. She yearned for the solitude. With a soothing touch, she pacified Alice's racing heart. Then, with a purposeful stride, she made her way to the bathroom, preparing to immerse them both in a sanctuary of warmth and tranquillity. Silently navigating the dimly lit corridor of the house, she felt a surge of relief wash over her as she discovered no trace of Otis's presence. As she leaned over the bath, her fingers reached out to insert the plug. In that very moment, a sudden, excruciating pain surged through her abdomen, as if a malevolent force had plunged a wicked blade into her unsuspecting flesh. She stood there; her face contorted in pain. It was no surprise to Jolene that poor Alice, her petite frame now stained with purple patches, was also in the throes of agony.

Jolene sprinkled Sea salt crystals into the bath, their glistening white forms dissolving into the warm water. A subtle fragrance filled the air as she carefully added a few drops of bleach solution to the water. The impending sting of their actions loomed ominously. They knew that in order to absolve themselves of their sins, they had to embark on a journey to cleanse their tainted souls. Never before had she experienced such a profound sense of filth and disgust. Lost in her own world, Alice entered the bathroom to find sanctuary with a hand towel, clutched tightly between her trembling thighs. As the bath was prepared, the two young girls approached it with caution, their movements synchronised as they eased themselves into the warm water simultaneously. Their tear-stained faces bore the marks of their shame, their resolve remained unyielding. With a shared determination, they started a ritualistic cleansing, their hands moving with a frenzied urgency.

 They meticulously scrubbed every inch of their bodies, as if attempting to wash away the sins that clung to their very souls. The air hung heavy with an unspoken understanding, not a word was uttered between them. In this solemn silence, they were hoping that the purifying waters would ease their hurt. The sound of running water filled the air, mingling with the tension that hung between them like a heavy fog. Jolene mustered the courage to break the suffocating silence. "I'm sorry," she whispered, her voice barely audible, above the steady stream. As they sat in the water, the bruises, dark and ominous, marred the delicate skin between their thighs, a haunting reminder to the brutality they had endured. Jolene winced, her body aching from the ordeal. Yet, her indomitable spirit, forged by years of enduring pain, shielded her from the worst of it. Poor Alice, with her delicate constitution, suffered far more acutely. The young girls remained motionless in the bathtub, their dainty frames filled with fear, plaintive cries echoing through the room. In a despairing attempt to find comfort in the darkness that surrounded them, they clung to one another, seeking a reprieve from their shared terror. Jolene's mind was filled with a chilling realisation, a haunting understanding of the horrors that had befallen them.

 They had been subjected to a series of brutal assaults; their vulnerable bodies rendered defenceless by the intoxicating haze that overpowered them. In their weakened state, resistance was futile, leaving them utterly helpless in the face of their assailant's relentless brutality. Jolene harboured a growing sense of unease, thoughts of this becoming a recurring incident plagued her mind. Leaning in close, she imparted her cautionary words to Alice, her voice a mere whisper, "Mark my words sis, under no circumstances will I allow this to happen again, I promise you." Alice's response was a mere nod, a subtle gesture that betrayed her inner turmoil. The words she longed to utter remained elusive, lost in her thoughts. The air was thick with the scent of sorrow. How could fate be so cruel, as to unleash a sinister twist of events on them on the very night they laid their beloved mother to rest?

In a chilling display of callous indifference, Otis had effortlessly demonstrated his complete disregard for the sisters. It was abundantly clear that they were destined to endure a harrowing existence, plagued by the relentless torment and anguish he would inflict upon them. Jolene emerged from the steaming bath. She gingerly wrapped a towel around herself, the fabric absorbing the remnants of her cleansing ritual. With a sense of duty, she extended a helping hand to her sister, who emerged from the water's soothing embrace. Together, they embarked on the task of drying Alice, their bond as sisters, evident in their tender movements. Jolene, gently dabbed at Alices wounds, her touch as tender as a whisper. Even during this gentle care, Alice's pained expressions betrayed the unrelenting agony she endured.

Jolene seethed with a fiery anger; her emotions ignited by the cruel hand of injustice that had befallen her. The world seemed to conspire against her, fuelling the flames of her fury. She stood there, her mind racing with uncertainty, yet her determination burned like a flame within her. The weight of the situation laid heavy on her shoulders, but she refused to succumb to despair. Deep down she knew that she had to rescue her innocent sister from the clutches of this malevolent nightmare. She found herself trapped in a web of helplessness, devoid of any viable options or trustworthy allies. The sisters were in a desolate state, abandoned by any hope of rescue. No saviours would emerge from the shadows, neither in the present nor in the distant future. They found themselves trapped in a relentless game of patience, their only way out was to hope for a future escape from the clutches of Otis. Once they were dressed, Jolene and Alice tip toed down to the kitchen, where Jolene set about making them a pot of sweet tea.

Fortunately, that night, Otis was nowhere to be seen. Jolene prepared dinner for herself and Alice, making sure to leave Otis's meal in the oven. As an act of defiance, she spat in his gravy, though it was a small act considering the circumstances. The girls were relieved in the knowledge that they wouldn't have to endure another night like the previous one. Alice asked Jolene to sleep with her in her bed, seeking comfort and safety. They huddled together on the single bed, holding each other as tight as their wounds would allow.

Throughout the night, Jolene was plagued by nightmares. Faces loomed over her, pawing at her. She recognised one of the men in her nightmare. He was the repulsive social worker, the very same one who allowed Otis to get guardianship over them. It confirmed her intuition, he had always made her skin crawl, now she knew why. The nightmares felt all too real, leaving her apprehensive about falling back to sleep. Jolene stayed awake, gently stroking Alice's hair, lost in her thoughts, desperately trying to formulate an escape plan. However, no viable options presented themselves. They were trapped, with nowhere to run or hide. Jolene contemplated the potential consequences of seeking help from social services, though that could lead to possible separation from Alice. She couldn't risk it. They needed time, time to heal, time to plan and time to gather their strength, both mentally and physically.

Desperate to protect her sister, Jolene considered striking a deal with Otis. Maybe if she earned enough money, the way her mother had, she could secure Alice's safety. Jolene would sacrifice herself, enduring the abuse, if it meant saving her sister. She prayed that Otis would accept her proposition. These thoughts swirled around her mind, as sunlight gradually filled the room. Jolene remained resolute in making things as bearable as possible for Alice, even if it meant sacrificing her own innocence to a string of men. She was determined to save her sister, knowing Alice couldn't endure the life Otis intended for them. Alice was delicate, always plagued by illness, and mentally slower than others. She had to be protected at all costs. The thought of losing her was unbearable. Jolene's mind raced, searching for a plan and someone to turn to for guidance. Maybe her mother's friend Maria could help.

As if in response to her thoughts, Maria burst through the door, smelling of cheap perfume with jangling copper bangles. Otis had sent her to check on the girls, ensuring they weren't too damaged from the previous night's ordeal. Maria, flawed as she was, emanated a sense of maternal concern as she fussed over the girls, inspecting them for bruises and tears. Jolene seized the opportunity and confided in Maria, pleading for a way to protect Alice from further harm. She was willing to do anything to safeguard her sister, even If it meant earning double what her mother did.

Maria empathized with Jolene's turmoil, agreeing that neither girl should have to live through such harm. But what could they do? Otis wouldn't listen to Maria either, he was a force unto himself. Jolene persisted, begging for Maria's help, so Maria reluctantly presented an idea. She suggested finding other girls their age to work for Otis, potentially from the local children's home. Jolene could establish friendships there, offering alternative targets for Otis's exploitation. The thought of sacrificing the innocence of others weighed heavily on Maria, but she saw it as a potential way to protect Alice. Overwhelmed with hope, tears streamed down Jolene's face as she contemplated Maria's proposal.

CHAPTER 3: Why didn't you die?

Jolene's moral compass wavered, but she felt the weight of responsibility for her sister's well-being. Maria gently wiped away Jolene's tears and offered a potential solution. She believed she could persuade Otis to consider the idea, knowing that the prospect of a significant financial gain might catch his attention. As long as Jolene was willing to go to great lengths to find these young girls for him, Maria thought this was a proposition that he wouldn't be able to turn down. Jolene's shame was evident, realising that these girls were someone else's daughters and sisters. She reasoned that perhaps they were already accustomed to the harsh realities of life, having grown up in the care system.

In a futile attempt to protect her sister, Jolene would only recruit girls who had already been exposed to the harsh realities of life. In her mind, it seemed like a win-win situation. The girls could earn some money, and Jolene could ensure her sister remained in the relative safety of the confines of their home, away from the dark path they were forced into. Saving her sister became Jolene's sole focus, overshadowing any consideration for her own safety or well-being. Alice was the only ray of light in her life now, and Jolene felt an overwhelming responsibility to shield her from further harm in the absence of their mother.

As Maria busied herself in the kitchen, preparing dinner for Otis and the girls, she received a call from him. Otis informed her that he was on his way home and expressed his hunger, expecting the girls to cater for him on his arrival. Maria, took the initiative and offered to cook for everyone, emphasizing that the girls were in no condition to attend to their stepfather's needs. Otis felt a twinge of annoyance, not wanting Maria to overstep her boundaries and assume their mother's role. On learning about Alice's fragile state following the previous night's traumatic events, he reluctantly saw reason and agreed to let Maria handle their dinner preparations, this time.

Maria was preparing Otis's favourite dish, jerk chicken. She knew how much he loved it and hoped that by pleasing his taste buds, she could gain favour with him. Maria had an ulterior motive, she wanted to show Otis the error of his ways. It wasn't fair for him to exploit the girls as his servants when she could take care of everything for him instead. She had once felt a tinge of jealousy towards the girl's mother. She had often believed that she should have been the one to marry Otis. Her inability to have children prevented their union, and Otis ended up marrying the girls' mother in the hope of having an heir. Otis had hidden his drug stash in the house which had inadvertently turned his wife into an addict, which had then in turn negated the chance of him ever having a son.

He quickly realised that his wife was no longer of any use to him, as she was consumed by her addiction. Without hesitation, he cast her out onto the streets to work for him. To him, she was just another worthless individual, a bottom feeder. He believed that once someone became a drug addict, they were forever trapped in that lifestyle. He showed no remorse for his role in her descent into addiction, refusing to acknowledge his own responsibility. The only positive aspect of his now deceased wife was her daughters. He intended to use and abuse them, ensuring that they earned him the money he required for a more luxurious lifestyle. As he found himself deep in debt with his suppliers, he saw the girls as a means to expand his control over the red-light district, and the drug trade. He harboured grand ambitions, and the sisters were his ticket to a lucrative empire.

As he drove home, his mind dominated by thoughts of making Alice pay for her fragility, he believed that the sisters owed him for everything he had done for them and their mother. In his twisted perspective, their mother had failed to repay him, it was now the girls' turn to bear the burden of his expectations. He had no regard for their well-being, happiness or safety, they were merely expendable assets to be used until they were depleted.

In an unexpected turn of events, as he passed through a green light, a violent impact shattered the side of his car. His body was thrown through the windscreen, landing broken and lifeless on the road. The piercing sound of sirens filled the air, followed by a sudden explosion. The consequences of his actions had finally caught up with him in a catastrophic instant.

Several weeks later, Otis regained consciousness after his coma. Weak and disoriented, he immediately demanded his phone, insisting on calling his best friend, and his 'girls' as he referred to them. The nurse attending to him was taken aback by his request, as she had observed that he hadn't had any visitors during his time in the hospital. It seemed that nobody cared about his condition, and she couldn't help but find the situation peculiar. There was an unsettling feeling that something was amiss, but she couldn't quite pinpoint it.

Concerned, the nurse went to the nurses' station to verify if his next of kin had been contacted. To her surprise, they had indeed attempted to reach out to his next of kin, who turned out to be his wife. Obviously, there had been no response. Returning to his room, the nurse gently explained that they had tried contacting his wife but received no answer. Otis's face drained of colour, he spat at the nurse, vehemently asserting that his wife was dead. According to him, she had passed away just before his car accident. The nurse stood there, stunned, realising that there was more to this story than met the eye.

Despite her reservations, the nurse decided to comply with Otis's request and fetched his phone. Curiosity got the better of her, and she wanted to see who he had asked to contact. Based on their brief interaction, she didn't get the impression that he was well-liked. There was something about him that screamed danger, and she had a knack for sensing trouble from a mile away.

The police were still investigating the details of Otis's car crash. The other driver involved in the accident had mysteriously disappeared, fuelling rumours among the hospital staff that Otis may have been the target of a deliberate hit. Whispers circulated throughout the ward, but nobody had concrete information about what had truly transpired. The nurse couldn't help but wonder if there was more to Otis's story than it seemed.

A few days later, during visiting hours, the nurse arrived for her shift and noticed that Otis had a visitor. The man was remarkably large, towering over Otis like a giant. She observed them engaged in a hushed conversation and couldn't resist the urge to eavesdrop. Casually pretending to read notes, she positioned herself near the door to catch snippets of their conversation. What she heard sent shockwaves through her.

Although she couldn't make out every word, she overheard that one of Otis's daughters was still bleeding, which somewhat explained their absence from the hospital. It seemed that a woman named Maria was taking looking after them. Otis's visitor revealed that he had been hunting down the driver responsible for the hit on Otis, but the police had already found the driver dead. There was also talk of another gang involved, as well as Otis's friend collecting money from his girls on the streets. The nurse scolded herself for listening in, realising that if Otis and his visitor discovered her, her own life might be in danger. She wondered what was meant by the alarming mention of one of his daughters still bleeding.

Trying to convince herself that she had misunderstood or misheard the conversation, she pushed the thoughts aside and continued with her shift. The nurse couldn't shake the nagging feeling that she should have reported what she had overheard to the authorities. Fear for her own safety kept her from taking any action, realising that sometimes things were better left untouched.

Back at Otis's home, both Jolene and Alice felt a sense of relief when they learned that he was hospitalised. They had secretly hoped for his death and had even prayed for it every night, desperate to escape his cruel grip. But fate had other plans, and Otis managed to survive. Despite their disappointment, they found solace in the fact that Maria had stepped in, to look after them.

Maria, bless her, had shouldered the responsibility of managing the household. During the day, she would look after the girls, providing them with care and support. At night, she would work the streets to make ends meet. Surprisingly, Maria had formed a close bond with the girls, which touched their hearts. They recognised that she genuinely cared for them. One particular incident stood out in Jolene's mind. Alice had suffered a tear and persistent bleeding, causing concern. Maria, resourceful as ever, had sought help from a client who happened to be a doctor. With his assistance, Alice's injuries were stitched up, and soon on the mend. Jolene was grateful that Maria had taken on a motherly role, offering them temporary respite and a sense of security.

CHAPTER 4: Time to heal.

Their newfound stability was short lived. The sister's spirits were dampened when they received news that Otis had emerged from his coma. The looming presence of their abusive stepfather cast a dark cloud over their lives once again.

At the hospital, Otis was being transferred to the rehabilitation unit. Due to his injuries, he had to relearn how to walk. He took comfort in knowing that his best friend had everything under control when it came to his affairs. Otis trusted Shady like a brother, since they had grown up together and had built his empire, side by side. Otis was determined to uncover the truth about who had ordered the hit on him. He had a hunch that it might be the gang he had been dealing with for his drug supply. Recently, they had added extra charges to his last batch, claiming he owed them more money. Although Otis had borrowed the drugs with some interest, the gang was continuously increasing the debt on a daily basis. He was angered by their unfair tactics, especially since the gang had become greedier ever since their patriarch had passed away, leaving the eldest sons in charge. This level of greed didn't sit well with Otis.

He vowed to confront them at the first opportune moment, already strategizing his next move in his mind. The aim was clear, he would impart a lasting lesson they would never be able to forget. Despite having had a mutually beneficial business association with their late father, it was imperative that he teach his sons a valuable and unforgettable lesson. Otis was preparing for an all-out conflict, resolved to make them suffer for their role in his accident. Who did they think they were, attempting to eliminate him? He would exact retribution for their deceit, ensuring they paid a heavy price, while also seizing control of their gang. For the time being, he needed to focus on regaining his health and mobility. Otis was determined to demonstrate his invincibility to everyone in his circle. They would pay dearly for their betrayal of what he considered to be an honourable agreement.

Back at the house, Jolene and Maria were relieved to see Alice's healing progress. For the first time since that dreadful night when they were drugged and raped, she had started laughing again. Night terrors had plagued Alice ever since, and she had been living in denial or at least pretending to be unaware of what had truly happened to her. Nonetheless, Alice found solace in the fact that the bleeding had ceased and the pain during urination had subsided.

On the other hand, Jolene seemed to bounce back from the events of that night relatively unscathed, which unsettled Maria. Jolene's trauma didn't appear to have any adverse effects on her, if anything, she seemed to mature beyond her years. She no longer behaved like a child but rather like a wise young woman, despite being only twelve years old.

Tomorrow would be Jolene's thirteenth birthday, and Maria had been secretly saving money to surprise the girls with a special outing. Despite Otis being hospitalised, Jolene had remained true to her word and managed to recruit girls from various children's homes, thanks to the help of Shady, her stepfather's trusted friend. Over forty young girls had been enlisted by Jolene, whom Shady referred to as "fresh meat." Shady hadn't yet informed Otis about these activities, but he constantly assured him that everything was under control, debts had been settled, and he had secured the next batch of drugs with an upfront payment.

Maria wanted to create a memorable experience for the sisters, for Jolene's Birthday. She had planned to take them to the cinema to watch the latest Disney film, followed by a visit to an indoor inflatable park, concluding with a celebratory meal. However, Maria hadn't anticipated Jolene's request to invite some of the recruited girls to her birthday party as well.

Maria tried to connect with all the girls Jolene had recruited, assuming a motherly role for them. But some of the girls seemed distant and had an air of cynicism about them, unlike Alice and Jolene. While Jolene had started working alongside the other girls, she only saw clients that Shady had picked out for her. Jolene justified her decision to Maria, explaining that when Otis returned, he would undoubtedly want her to work for him, so she might as well get accustomed to it early on. Jolene also found it easier to recruit new girls by joining them at the parties.

Jolene genuinely valued the friendships she had formed with the girls she recruited. They admired her, and she, with Shady's assistance, ensured their well-being. Jolene made it clear that no clients were allowed to harm the girls under their care.

Shady, despite being known as the tough guy for Otis, lacked the intellect to handle everything on his own. He relied on Maria and Jolene's assistance, recognising that he couldn't sort out the situation for Otis without their help. Shady had always felt a sense of responsibility towards Jolene and her late mother, and he believed it was his duty to try and protect them.

While Shady held a deep and unwavering love and loyalty for Otis, he couldn't ignore his disdain for how Otis treated his women. Shady, who cherished his own mother, couldn't fathom behaving so wickedly towards women. Therefore, he made it a point to assist Otis's girls whenever possible, taking it upon himself to resolve any issues before involving Otis. Whenever one of the girls was robbed or experienced an overdose, Otis would ruthlessly beat them before pursuing the dealer or client responsible. However, Shady, would solely focus on seeking retribution against the dealer or client who harmed one of the girls. Shady felt a sense of concern about the current dynamics, because he knew Otis would not listen to a woman, and their involvement could potentially jeopardize everything they had worked for in an attempt to please Otis. This was precisely why Shady withheld specific details from Otis. Despite not being the brightest individual, when it came to understanding Otis, Shady knew him all too well.

Jolene's Birthday party was a resounding success. Providing a temporary respite from the impending return of the dark cloud that would darken their world, when Otis returned from rehab, at least a month away. Jolene received a beautiful necklace with a cross pendant from Maria, and even Shady had gifted her a silver dolphin bangle. The inflatable park brought immense joy to all the girls, and they concluded the day with a dinner at Poppins restaurant, where Jolene indulged in her favourite chocolate flake pancakes. Jolene's mother and Alice used to frequent the restaurant before her mother became involved with Otis. While Alice initially felt melancholic at the cinema due to the presence of the other girls, she soon perked up at the inflatable park.

Maria was delighted that the day went smoothly, as the girls were gradually becoming like a large family to her. She found herself loving each and every one of them, despite their distinct qualities. Some had a more acquired taste and were a bit brash, but today's experience reminded Maria that, in the end, they were all young girls who had lost a significant portion of their childhood. The girls held a genuine affection for Jolene, viewing her as a big sister, while Shady had become an uncle figure to them all. Maria's only concern lay with Otis and how he would handle the situation when he returned home. Would he instil fear in them, rendering their hard work futile? Or would he accept the new dynamics within his specific business affairs.

Maria believed it was essential to devise a plan with Shady and Jolene for when Otis returned. They would have to sell the idea to him. Without their planning and expertise, Otis would have lost everything. Jolene's hard work had saved him, his home, and alleviated his debts. If only they could find a way to make Otis understand that handling younger girls required a gentler approach, that they needed to be treated with more kindness than he was capable of providing.

The following evening, as Jolene and Maria prepared for work, they sat down at the table to discuss the imminent return of Otis and how they could potentially convince him to adopt a more lenient approach. Jolene contemplated whether doubling the size of their team of young girls would convince Otis to leave that aspect of his business to Shady. They both acknowledged that, as women, Otis would never listen to their plans. Therefore, they considered the possibility of persuading Shady to speak to Otis, presenting the idea as his own. They would emphasize that these girls needed a father figure to look after them, and that Otis could risk damaging the business, and driving the girls away, if he treated them as he did his adult street workers. They would need to make a point of informing Otis of the potential scrutiny from professionals, at the care home institutions if the girls started showing signs of physical abuse. Jolene had been regimented in keeping the girls clean and ensuring they were free from beatings. Although they had a few care home managers in their pockets, even they admitted that they wouldn't be able to prevent further investigations if the girls started appearing in poor condition.

"It's settled then. I'll do my best to double the number of girls working for us. Once that's done, we just need to get Shady on board. He can tell Otis that it was his idea and emphasize how happy the girls are, and how much money they're earning," Jolene declared confidently.

Maria nodded in agreement but voiced her concern, "But how will you find more girls? There are no more children's homes nearby." Jolene revealed her resourcefulness, informing Maria that she had already selected certain girls from their team to recruit others at their schools. Maria was both impressed and apprehensive, as recruiting girls from stable homes seemed risky. As she voiced her worries to Jolene, she later dismissed them and explained that they would only target girls from broken families living in poverty on council estates. These girls were already on the brink of entering the care system themselves, and they would appreciate the financial support, gifts, and the feeling of being special. Maria found it difficult to argue with Jolene, considering her own background as part of a lineage of working girls and having started in the industry herself at a tender age. As long as they could keep Otis away from these girls, they stood a better chance of earning an extra income and staying safe from harm.

Jolene recognised the immense effort required to enlist the council estate girls into their operations. She would have to train some of her trusted girls to become recruiters themselves. She knew that at least six of them had the potential to excel in this role. However, her goal was to have a presence in every school in the area, so she would need to put in extra effort with some of the girls who she considered partially capable of recruiting. Growing up in poverty had armed them with the necessary tools. Girls craved attention, they enjoyed feeling special, and the prospect of earning an extra income would be very enticing to them. Jolene planned to explain to the girls that these clients were like 'paying boyfriends', and she would organize the parties, where they would be well taken care of. Most girls desired money for new clothes, makeup, and occasionally drugs. Jolene preferred not to have girls on her team who used hard drugs. While she didn't mind if they drank or smoked a bit of weed, she viewed hard drugs as a dangerous pursuit. She understood that girls with drug habits might be easier to recruit, as they would need the money to sustain their addiction. She already had around ten girls on the books who were heavy drug users. In those cases, she would have Shady supply their drugs to ensure they were clean and minimise the risk of overdose.

Every evening followed a routine in their household. Jolene would set out at 3pm to recruit new girls from various schools in the area. After the recruitment drives, she would take the newly recruited girls to prearranged parties. Jolene would engage in activities with them, to help them feel more comfortable and then leave in the early hours. Appointing one of her trustworthy girls to oversee the party, with the assistance of a doorman provided by Shady, to ensure the girls' safety. Jolene would arrive home so that Maria could then go to work on the streets. This arrangement ensured that Alice was never left alone at home. During the day, Maria and Jolene took on the responsibility of home educating Alice. It proved to be a challenging task as Alice had difficulty grasping most subjects. Surprisingly though, Alice discovered a passion for their mother's old sewing machine. She taught herself to create dresses and curtains, showcasing remarkable skill. Despite her talent with the sewing machine, Alice constantly struggled with reading and writing.

Jolene and Maria ensured that Alice had everything she needed for her dressmaking pursuits, providing her with an ample supply of materials. Jolene was close to reaching her recruitment target, resulting in a significant increase in their income. They now had added a total of fifty-three girls to the forty-two already working for them, each earning over two hundred pounds per week. Shady had successfully arranged a consistent flow of clients for the parties, allowing each girl to earn a hundred pounds for themselves. With their unwavering determination and astute business acumen, Maria and Shady triumphantly transformed their enterprise, yielding a remarkable weekly profit of five thousand pounds once all necessary expenses had been dutifully settled. Additionally, the doorman received an extra hundred pounds for their services. The house had been transformed with new curtains made by Alice, adding to the overall positive atmosphere. Life seemed to be going well for everyone.

Shady was genuinely impressed by Jolene's skills in the business. She excelled at recruiting young girls effortlessly, a talent that came naturally to her. While he felt a pang of sadness that Jolene had chosen to follow her mother's path, he understood that Otis would have eventually forced her into the same line of work. He surprised himself by agreeing to Maria and Jolene's terms, knowing that he would have to lie to Otis. Their priority now was to keep Alice away from the destructive influence of Otis to protect everything that was still pure in their lives.

CHAPTER 5: The Devils at the door.

Maria's heart sank as she received the call informing her that Otis was on his way home. She knew she had to act quickly, and immediately phoned Jolene to inform her of the situation. It was decided that Jolene should be present when Otis arrived, so they could face him together. The news cast a shadow of uncertainty over the room, causing both Maria and Alice to halt their activities. Maria understood that need to prioritise putting Alice at ease, before focusing on finishing the bookkeeping in time for Otis's return. The thought of her stepfather's return had already begun to unsettle Alice. Alice was scared and Maria wanted to provide as much comfort and support as possible to help her through it. Shady had said they would be home at 5pm.

Leaving one of her top girls in charge, Jolene's mind was in turmoil as she rushed home in the taxi. The news of Otis's imminent return had shaken her to the core. She couldn't help but feel a mixture of fear and anxiety, knowing all too well the kind of man he was. Jolene had witnessed his violent tendencies and his disdain for women first hand, she dreaded the thought of having to face him again. She desperately hoped that the success and profitability of their enterprise would be enough to sway Otis's actions and protect Alice from his wrath. The thought of her sister being subjected to his abuse was unbearable, and Jolene was determined to do everything in her power to shield her.

As the taxi ferried her closer to home, Jolene's mind raced with thoughts and plans. She knew she had to remain composed and present, and they needed to show a united front with Maria and Shady when confronting Otis. Perhaps if they emphasized the financial gains and stability they had achieved, he would see the value in allowing them to continue their work without interference. Deep down, Jolene hoped that Otis could set aside his cruelty and recognize the efforts they had made to build a successful business. She held on to the slim hope that he would prioritize the financial benefits and be willing to let them continue their operations unhindered. But as the taxi sped towards home, Jolene couldn't shake off the overwhelming sense of unease and uncertainty that loomed over her.

Maria had just put Alice to bed. It had been too much for the poor girl, who had cried herself to sleep in Maria's arms. As Maria entered the kitchen and put the kettle on, she jumped in surprise when Jolene walked in. Seeing it was only Jolene, Maria's face softened, and she said, "Let me finish these books, they'll keep Otis off our backs. I just need ten more minutes, and then we can talk, okay?" Jolene nodded, understanding the importance of completing the books. She quietly made her way to Alice's room, giving her sister a loving kiss and stroking her face without waking her. Jolene closed the door gently and returned downstairs with a heavy heart. Maria had prepared tea for both of them and was about to start making dinner for Otis when Jolene whispered, "Just stop, please. I need to know what we're going to do. Let's order dinner in and say it's to celebrate his homecoming."

Maria nodded in agreement, setting the kettle aside. She joined Jolene at the table, taking a moment to collect her thoughts. "Okay, Jolene, we need a plan," she said firmly. "We've worked so hard to build this business and protect the girls. We can't let Otis come in and ruin everything." Jolene's eyes were fixed on Maria, filled with anticipation. Maria continued, "First, we need to present a united front. We have to make Otis see that everything is running smoothly and that we've been successful in his absence. The books will help with that." Jolene let out a sigh of relief, grateful that Maria had been handling the bookkeeping. She felt a glimmer of hope with the knowledge that they had concrete evidence of their financial success. "Secondly," Maria went on, "we need to stress the importance of the girls and their well-being. We can't let Otis mistreat them or jeopardize their safety. We have to make him understand that the girls are our priority." Jolene nodded, her determination shining through. "I've been thinking about proposing a partnership with Shady," she said. "We can tell Otis that Shady has taken over the management of the younger girls. We'll explain that they need a more caring approach, and Shady is the right person for the job."

Maria considered Jolene's suggestion and nodded in agreement. "That might work," she said. "If we make it clear that Shady's involvement is to protect the girls and ensure their well-being, maybe Otis will be more willing to accept it."

Taking a sip of her tea, Jolene's mind raced with ideas and possibilities. "And we'll emphasize our financial success," she added. "We'll show him the numbers, the profits we've made. Hopefully, that will convince him to leave us alone." Maria reached out, placing a reassuring hand on Jolene's. "We'll do everything we can to keep Alice safe and ensure our business continues," she said firmly. "We've come this far, and we won't let Otis destroy it all." Jolene nodded, determination flickering in her eyes. They had faced challenges before, and they would face this one together. They would protect their girls and find a way to navigate the dangers that awaited them when Otis returned. Shortly after their discussion, Shady appeared with Otis in a wheelchair.

Jolene and Maria exchanged nervous glances as Shady presented the books to Otis. The room fell silent as Otis slowly perused the financial records before him. His eyes darted back and forth, scrutinizing the numbers, and a faint smirk formed on his face. "Well, well," Otis said, his voice dripping with sarcasm. "Looks like my girls have been busy behind my back." Jolene and Maria held their breath, waiting for his response. They knew Otis could be unpredictable, and they braced themselves for his reaction. After what felt like an eternity, Otis finally spoke again. "I must admit, I'm impressed," he said with a hint of grudging admiration in his tone. "You've done well girls. You've exceeded my expectations." Jolene and Maria exchanged relieved glances, the tension in the room easing slightly. Perhaps their plan was working after all.

Otis continued, "And these parties, you say. Young girls from care homes and schools, clever move Jolene. Expanding our clientele and keeping things discreet." Jolene's voice was steady as she replied, "yes, Dad. We saw an opportunity and took it. The girls are earning good money, and we've ensured their safety and well-being." Maria chimed in, her voice filled with determination, "we've created a strong network, Otis. The girls trust us, and they're happy with their work. We've built something profitable, something we can all benefit from." Otis leaned back in his wheelchair, with a calculating glint in his eyes. "I have to say, I didn't see this coming," he admitted. "But I'm not one to turn down success. You've proven yourselves." Jolene and Maria exchanged another glance, with a mixture of relief and cautious hope in their eyes. It seemed their efforts to protect the girls and secure their own future had made an impression on him. Otis raised an eyebrow, his tone changing slightly. "But don't think this means you can run the show without me," he warned. "I may be impressed, but I'm still in charge. I'll oversee the operations, and you'll report to me." Jolene and Maria nodded in understanding. They knew they couldn't escape Otis's control entirely, but they had gained some leverage and earned a certain degree of autonomy.

As Shady poured the tea, the room filled with a mixture of relief and cautious optimism. The battle was far from over, but Jolene and Maria had made significant progress. They had managed to impress Otis, gain his begrudging approval, and secure their place in the business. As they sat down to share the meal from Mamas Jerk Chicken Kitchen, Jolene and Maria knew that their journey was far from over. They would continue to protect the girls, navigate the complexities of their world, and find ways to outmanoeuvre Otis while keeping Alice safe from harm. But for now, they allowed themselves a moment of respite, savouring the taste of victory and hoping that their newfound strength would be enough to protect their empire and those they cared for. That evening, Shady remained on the sofa in Otis's bedroom, assisting Otis. Maria, as usual, went off to work in the early hours, demonstrating her commitment. She wanted to prove to Otis that the household was generating an income, including her contributions. However, if she were honest with herself, she also craved some personal space. The streets felt like her true home, where she felt at ease. In comparison, her current life seemed overly complicated. Working in the red-light district, she only had to look out for herself and could easily spot suspicious clients. Life there was simpler, and something was bothering her. Otis was too easily influenced this time, even offering a backhanded compliment to herself and Jolene, which was completely out of character. She had a dreadful feeling that Otis had ulterior motives, that he would revert to his usual self-serving and deceitful ways, causing chaos for everyone. His ego would be wounded, as they had done an exceptional job. The thought sent a shiver down her spine, but for tonight, she resolved to set aside her concerns and focus on earning a substantial amount of money to please Otis.

While Otis was still recovering at home, Jolene, Maria and Shady were extremely cautious about their behaviour around him. They had to take turns meeting outside the house to discuss business matters privately, which made things challenging as one of them always had to be home to look after Alice and attend to Otis. Otis had now progressed to using crutches and was able to move around the house, often accompanied by Shady.

Shady wanted to show off their new office space to Otis. The business had expanded to the point where running everything from home was no longer feasible. Shady and Maria had taken the initiative to secure a portacabin as an office space, for their growing empire. They also saw it as an opportunity to keep Otis away from home and Alice for longer periods. Alice had become quiet since Otis returned, she spent her time sewing, and had started refusing home learning sessions with Maria and Jolene. Occasionally, Otis would attempt to engage Alice in conversation, only to have her burst into tears and retreat to her bedroom. This frustrated him, but fortunately, one of the household members was always there to calm him down. It was Shady who spoke up, saying, "she's just a child Otis. She's been through a lot, and it has made her more fragile than ever. Give her some time." Otis took note of this reprimand, storing it for future reference. He felt that this group was becoming too comfortable with telling him what to do in his own house. He vowed to make them suffer greatly once he was back to full strength.

Unbeknown to Maria, Shady and Jolene, Otis was brewing a sinister plan to regain control of his businesses. He was determined to teach them all a lesson for daring to think they could dictate to him. His physical limitations following the crash prevented him from going it alone and taking any immediate action. Otis was usually not one to wait.

Three months had passed with no leads on the whereabouts of the rival gang. But once he regained his mobility, Otis planned to seek them out and unleash an all-out war. The two brothers responsible for ordering the hit on him were reportedly in Trinidad, and Otis intended to exact revenge for every offense, repaying them for their actions. Shady, Maria and Jolene would have to wait. As for young Alice, she would be the last on his list. Otis had ample time to contemplate and strategize while confined to his broken body. Although his legs were weakened and damaged, his mind remained sharp. He utilized this time to quietly plan his next moves, desiring to reclaim everything that belonged to him. He aimed to demonstrate that he was still a formidable force. It wouldn't be long before he could take back what was rightfully his. He would show these women who the true boss was, ensuring that no one would ever dare to cross him again. The new recruits that Jolene had brought in were oblivious to his true nature, thus, he needed to reveal his identity and assert his dominance. Otis would arrange a meeting with all of them, carefully assessing who could be used to his advantage. His deep-seated animosity towards his family and all women fuelled his drive to regain control.

CHAPTER 6: Always watching.

Jolene felt a sense of satisfaction with how things had turned out. Otis had actually left them all alone to handle their affairs, she wondered if the accident had changed him in any way. Only time would tell. She had no intention of dwelling on him today. One of her top girls had informed her that another girl had been charging extra for unprotected sex. Jolene was furious. It wasn't one of her girls from the care homes, it was a girl from the council estates, named Lorna. Ever since Lorna had joined their group, she had been nothing but trouble. On a couple of occasions, she had attempted to take clients from parties to her own home, but fortunately, the vigilant doormen had prevented it. Jolene and Shady had sternly warned her about the dangers of such actions. Moreover, Lorna had been caught trying to introduce drugs to the other girls, pushing Jolene's patience to the limit. This time, her recklessness had resulted in contracting chlamydia. Jolene considered Lorna fortunate that her actions had only led to a mild STD and not something more life-altering like HIV or herpes. But this was the final straw. Jolene decided to accompany Lorna to the clinic for her STD medication, after which she would deliver the news that Lorna was no longer welcome as part of the team.

 The G.U.M. clinic served as a regular destination for all the girls, providing free sexual health care whilst ensuring their personal information remained confidential. It was an essential measure for Jolene to keep her girls healthy and safe. Additionally, the clinic offered the added benefit of distributing large packets of eighteen or more free condoms to each girl on every visit. Jolene couldn't help but look forward to removing Lorna from the team. The girl had caused far more trouble than she was worth, and Jolene strongly suspected that Lorna had resorted to injecting heroin between her toes. Lorna frequently showed up to parties completely out of it, exhibiting the unmistakable signs Jolene had observed during her mother's heavy drug use. Jolene didn't want Lorna dragging the other girls down to her level. After today, Lorna would have to find her own path in life. Jolene's anger simmered within her. She had treated Lorna like family, just like all her other girls, but it never seemed enough for Lorna. She always craved more money and attention than the rest. It seemed as though Lorna was on a self-destructive path, caring little about anything or anyone, including herself.

JOLENE'S OTHER GIRLS all came from troubled backgrounds, but they understood the importance of their situation. Jolene made it a priority to take care of them as best she could. However, a lingering worry remained in her mind, the fear that Otis would come back into their lives and wreak havoc once he fully recovered. The doctors had informed Otis that he would walk with a permanent limp, there was no further treatment available beyond the pins and plates that had saved his legs. In moments like these, Jolene couldn't help but feel betrayed by God. She questioned why, if God truly cared, Otis hadn't perished in the crash. Her mother had always made them pray at bedtime, but now Jolene found herself blaming God for her mother's death and for Otis surviving. Out of respect for her mother's wishes, she still uttered prayers each night, but her faith had been shattered by recent events.

Jolene stood outside the G.U.M. clinic, waiting for a taxi to take her home, a whirlwind of thoughts swirling in her mind. She had delivered the unfortunate news to Lorna, who responded with screams and threats. Jolene paid her off and sent her away, disregarding Lorna's outburst. She knew it was imperative that Shady located Lorna later in order to have a serious talk with her, to make sure she understood the importance of keeping quiet. The last thing they needed was that troublesome girl, threatening to expose them to the police. It would only take one foolish act to bring unwanted attention their way. So far, they had managed to operate discreetly, keeping the parties low-key and the girl's content. But Lorna posed a real risk, and although Jolene didn't want any harm to come to her, it was necessary to be firm with her, to make it clear that she had crossed a line.

The following day brought devastating news that shook the ground beneath them. The headline blared, 'Police Investigating Murder of Teenager Suspected of Involvement in the Red-Light District.' Maria's blood ran cold as she heard the report on the television. Just the night before, she had spotted Lorna in her neighbourhood and desperately tried to warn her, urging her to go home as she was too young for such dangerous activities. But Lorna had defiantly dismissed her, flipping her middle finger in the air as she disappeared from Maria's sight. Now, sitting at the kitchen table, Maria knew she had to inform Shady and Jolene. Shady was at the new offices with Otis when he received the call. He couldn't believe the words that reached his ears. It finally made sense why he hadn't been able to locate Lorna after Maria had reached out to him the previous evening. Maria had given Shady the information, hoping he would intervene and have a serious conversation with the young girl, but Lorna had vanished without a trace. It now appeared that she had fallen victim to a tragic fate, presumably at the hands of a dangerous client.

As Shady hung up the phone, a sly smile crept across Otis's face, and he taunted, "What was that about? Has the cat got your tongue, or did the cat take someone else's tongue?" Shady slumped into the office chair, dreading the conversation he was about to have with Otis. With a heavy sigh, he began, "Jolene had to let go of one of the girls yesterday. Let's just say she was causing trouble for your business. Well, Maria just called to inform me that the police are investigating the murder of a young girl, and she believes it could be Lorna, the girl we let go." Otis's knowing smile persisted, leaving Shady with an uneasy feeling. Otis interjected, "Look, if the girl was causing problems, then whoever killed her did us a favour." Shady understood the logic, but he couldn't shake the belief that the girl didn't deserve such a fate. Regardless, he kept his thoughts to himself.

"Listen, if the police are searching for her murderer, we're in the clear. Everyone knows the dangers of the red-light district, especially for kids. Some clients can get carried away and go too far, that's all it'll be." Shady remained silent, but he couldn't shake off the chilling callousness of Otis's words.

Jolene burst through the door of the family home, her eyes filled with panic, as she rushed into the kitchen, startling Alice who pricked her finger on the sewing machine. "Is it true?" Jolene shrieked, desperation lacing her voice. "Please, Maria, tell me it's not true." Overwhelmed with emotion, she collapsed into a chair at the table, tears streaming down her high cheekbones. Maria hurried over to embrace her, offering comfort. "Yes, it's true," Maria confirmed. "Lorna has been murdered. I received a call from one of our contacts in the police force. They couldn't provide any more details for now, but they promised to keep me informed. Jolene, it's not your fault. We did our best for her; she had a self-destructive streak." Jolene sat there, paler than usual, silently shedding tears. Maria couldn't bear to see her so devastated. She knew Jolene would blame herself for letting Lorna go, but there had been no other viable option. Lorna had sealed her own fate, now she had paid the ultimate price. Lorna's lifeless body had been discovered in a park, unclothed, brutally beaten, and with her tongue removed. Maria made a silent vow to shield Jolene from the gruesome details. She was determined to protect her from any further anguish, even if it meant carrying that burden herself.

 Maria had reached out to the other young girls who were part of their operation, not only to gather information about the rumours surrounding Lorna's death, but also to provide reassurance and ensure that business would continue as usual. She emphasized that the top girls, along with the doormen at the parties, would be in charge. Maria was adamant that Jolene needed the night off, as she was in no condition to work. Meanwhile, Alice having tended to her injured finger, had returned to the kitchen and sensed the heaviness in the air. Although she couldn't fully grasp the gravity of the situation, seeing her sister's tears prompted her to offer a comforting hug. As Alice, Jolene and Maria huddled together for support, Otis and Shady entered the house.

 As the two men made their entrance into the kitchen, Otis wore a sinister grin, relishing in the turmoil he had created. This was only the beginning of his plan, to break them down, undermine their capabilities and exploit their emotional vulnerabilities. The doctor had given him the green light to travel to Trinidad within two weeks, he would be accompanied by paid guns who would eliminate the brothers responsible for his accident. He intended to savour his revenge on these women and Shady. He wanted to meticulously dismantle them over time, deriving pleasure from watching them suffer from the side lines. His plan for them could wait. Seating himself at the table with an air of authority, Otis spoke with a demanding tone, "Maria, make us some coffee. The girls will be fine. Jolene, this is not your fault, and you know it. That girl made bad choices; her demise was inevitable. Pull yourself together. You wanted to be a part of my business, didn't you? Well, toughen up girl." Jolene felt her ears burn with the scathing reprimand. It was as if venom had been spat into them. She now understood more than ever that Otis would never truly love anyone, not even her or her sister. He would always shift the blame onto others, absolving himself of any responsibility for his actions.

    The kitchen was enveloped in a heavy silence as everyone in the room recognized the need to tread cautiously around Otis, aware of his potential explosive temperament. Maria placed two coffees on the table for Otis and Shady, then poured herself and the girls another cup of tea. It was in this tense atmosphere that Jolene bravely broke the silence, speaking up with a tentative voice, "I promise to try harder Dad. I want to follow in your footsteps and make you proud of me." Otis's grin widened, feeling a surge of satisfaction as Jolene not only referred to him as Dad but expressed her desire to be mentored by him. It stroked his ego, and in that moment, he softened slightly, a rare occurrence in his life. He pondered the enigma that was Jolene, a young girl who seemed wise beyond her years. Perhaps he would temporarily postpone his plans and see how this played out. If he could shape her into a reflection of himself, she might prove to be a valuable asset. Otis resolved to think deeply about this opportunity. Though he harboured a deep disdain for women in general, Jolene stood out as an intriguing anomaly.

CHAPTER 7: Mechanism of Control.

Jolene rose from her seat, realising it was time to tuck Alice into bed. Sensing that Alice appeared even more fragile than usual, she attributed it to the events of the day. The two of them ascended the stairs, seeking solace and privacy. Kneeling beside Alice's bed, they joined in prayer. Unexpectedly, Alice included a plea for God to watch over Lorna. Jolene couldn't help but feel unsettled by Alice's words, sensing that her sister knew more than she was letting on. With a tender touch, Jolene tucked Alice into bed, planting a kiss on her forehead. She leaned in and whispered into Alice's ear, "I love you, but to keep you safe, will you please try to hug Otis, especially at bedtime? And will you please start calling him Dad for me. Promise me, Alice." Alice extended her hand, pinkie finger extended, and replied, "pinkie promise."

Jolene felt a sense of relief, giving Alice another gentle kiss before quietly closing the bedroom door behind her. As she descended the stairs and re-entered the kitchen, she was surprised to find the adults laughing and sharing light-hearted stories. Shady's anecdotes about his mother brought a sense of joy and ease to the room. Maria, busy at the stove, served the men their dinner. Everything seemed harmonious and right with the world. Jolene recognized the need to put the incident with Lorna behind her, not only to please Otis but also to preserve the rare moments of laughter and happiness that had been scarce since his return from the hospital. She didn't want to dampen the mood. Putting on a brave face, Jolene joined in their camaraderie. She was determined to do whatever it took to win Otis over, knowing that it was the key to her and Alice's survival. Otis would soon be out of their lives, bound for Trinidad on a plane. Jolene reasoned that she could maintain a favourable relationship with him until then. Although she had never travelled abroad, she had heard Shady's stories about Trinidad, a place of both beauty and danger. In a fleeting moment, a small voice in Jolene's mind found itself wishing for Otis not to return from his trip.

In the following weeks, time seemed to stand still, but eventually the day arrived for Shady to accompany Otis to the airport. The police had conducted some investigations into Lorna's murder, but their efforts had yielded no significant leads. It appeared that unless a serial killer was on the loose, her death had lost its importance. There had been no further incidents in the red-light district.

Just as Shady and Otis were about to leave the house, Otis reminded the girls that Shady was in charge during his absence. Despite his resentment toward Shady's close relationship with the household, Otis still trusted him. In Trinidad, Otis had enlisted the help of old friends to track down the two brothers responsible for his ordeal. Otis had made a solemn vow to personally exact his revenge. He planned to subject the brothers to unimaginable torment, ensuring they suffered slow and agonising deaths. The only inconvenience he faced was airport security, as he couldn't bring his tool bag along. Otis made arrangements to obtain a new one during his trip. Inside that bag lay a collection of torture tools, waiting to be deployed. After completing his vengeful task, Otis intended to dispose of the men's lifeless bodies in the Caribbean Sea, leaving their remains to become food for the sharks. He would also cast his tools to the depths of the ocean. The anticipation of inflicting suffering upon the brothers filled Otis with a twisted sense of delight. It had been a while since he had truly indulged in such sadistic acts, aside from the incident with the girl, which he considered insignificant compared to what awaited the two brothers.

Shrouded in an air of secrecy, Shady and Otis engaged in conversation as they traversed the dimly lit streets speeding toward the airport. Their words, laden with hidden meanings and veiled intentions. With every step, their words echoed the rhythm of their illicit dealings. The neon glow of the airport sign flickered in the distance. The air was thick with tension as Otis, a man known for his demanding nature, revealed his true intentions. Shady, a hardened individual with a past shrouded in mystery, found himself taken aback by the words that escaped Otis's lips. The shockwaves reverberated through Shady's very being, penetrating the depths of his soul. As the words came from Otis's lips, it was a command wrapped in a veil of authority. "Inform Jolene and Maria," he began, his voice low and domineering, "that I expect them to double up on the workload whilst I am away. I have left a document at the office. A list of the various care homes scattered throughout the neighbouring boroughs, accompanied by a map detailing a forty-mile radius. This circle, is a visual representation of my grand plan, it reveals the precise areas where our expansion efforts are to be focused."

In the dimly lit car, a cloud of smoke hung heavy in the air as Otis leaned back in the worn leather car seat, smoking a spliff. "Maria will also help to expand my empire, recruiting more women to join the ranks of my adult street girls." The red-light district, his domain of debauchery and vice, needed an influx of fresh faces to satisfy his insatiable desires of expansion. Maria held the key to this dark endeavour. "I wish for Maria, to procure no less than ten additional women for our inventory. The streets hunger for new temptations, and we must satisfy her cravings." His mind was a twisted labyrinth of wicked schemes, as Otis spoke of Jolene. "As for Jolene," he mused, a sly smile playing upon his lips, "she and her girls shall work tirelessly on a mission to expand our reach, scouring the other twelve care homes on my list for fresh meat."

Shady had a flicker of doubt dance within his troubled mind. Should he dare voice his concerns to Otis, as his loyal confidante? The stakes were high, and the consequences dire. Shady's heart raced, torn between the desire for power and the fear of betrayal. His voice was filled with concern, a hint of desperation seeping through the words. "Otis," he began, his eyes narrowing as he leaned in closer, "don't you reckon that the burden might be too weighty for a mere slip of a girl? She's but thirteen, after all." With a sinister smirk, Otis shot back, his voice dripping with contempt, "She claims she yearns to earn my admiration; this is how she will please me. I demand that every detail be executed to perfection before my arrival. Should either of them dare to disappoint me, they shall face dire consequences..." Otis's voice, like a whisper carried by the wind, gradually faded into the abyss of silence. Shady's senses tingled with an eerie anticipation, his instincts honed from years of navigating the treacherous characteristics of Otis. He refused to lend an ear to the ominous words that hung in the air, for he recognised them for what they truly were, a murderous threat, not a veiled threat. Shady knew there would be no negotiating with him.

After bidding farewell to Otis at the airport, Shady drove back to Otis's home, his mind preoccupied with the dilemma before him. He was uncertain about how to break the news to Maria and Jolene without instilling fear in them. He also worried about the potential trouble Otis's insatiable greed could cause. Shady realised he would need to hire a driver for Jolene, enabling her to travel across the city and expand into other areas. The workload was overwhelming for a young girl. Shady admitted to himself that he wasn't cut out for this type of responsibility, he was more of a muscle man than a strategist. He decided to see what Maria and Jolene had to say. They were the masterminds, while he played a supporting role. They would need to find a way to make it all work. Shady had faith in Maria's resourcefulness and was impressed by Jolene's natural aptitude and shrewdness in the business. Though it weighed heavily on Jolene's heart to involve young girls in this line of work, it was all she had known since her mother became involved with Otis. Even before that, Jolene's mother had been best friends with Maria, so it was inevitable that Jolene would learn from their experiences. Amidst these challenges, there was a silver lining, they would all be free from Otis's presence for the next two weeks.

Shady decided that the best course of action was to gather Jolene, Maria, and Alice and bring them to their newly acquired offices at the reclamation yard, where Otis had left the list and map. He called Maria, to inform them that he would be picking them up, and to be ready when he beeped his horn outside their house.

Maria couldn't shake off her nervousness after receiving Shady's call. Something felt off, as it was unusual for Shady to request that they all leave the house together with him. His dismissive tone during the phone call heightened her unease. Maria's intuition told her that it had something to do with Otis. Although he would be on his way to Trinidad by now, she was certain he had given instructions to Shady.

"Come on Alice, let's get you ready to go," Maria said, catching Jolene's curious gaze. Jolene asked Maria what was happening and where they were going. Maria simply shrugged and explained what Shady had conveyed during the call. Jolene packed her belongings, as did Maria and Alice, then they patiently waited for Shady's arrival.

During the car ride to the offices, Shady remained tight-lipped. He didn't provide them with any further information, only stating that everything would become clear once they reached Otis's offices. The night was cold and rainy, and Alice grew hungry as none of them had eaten dinner yet.

On arriving at the offices, they all sat down, eager to hear what Shady had to say. He revealed that Otis wanted them to intensify their recruitment efforts. Jolene was tasked with recruiting from areas beyond their borough, and Shady presented her with a list of care homes to consider. As for Maria, Otis expected her to recruit a minimum of ten new women for his territory in the red-light district. Maria let out a whistle in response, remarking on the relative ease of her task compared to Jolene's.

Realising that they had no choice in the matter, Maria said, "well, I guess Jolene will have to ask some of our more senior girls from the parties to assist with recruitment. Each girl would need to take responsibility for two care homes. Perhaps we can manage with a smaller team. It will mean less girls at the party houses, but I don't see any other option. We have to meet the targets set by Otis; we can't risk failing." Jolene was grateful for Maria's sharp thinking in the midst of her shock and disbelief. She was already so tired, she barely had time to eat let alone catch her breath. Her body often hurt after the parties. She hoped it would get easier, that her body wouldn't let her down. But even after months of her body being used to please the men at the parties, it still hurt. But it would all be worth it, to save her sister. Throughout the discussion, Alice sat at the table, engrossed in scribbling on a piece of paper, seemingly unaware of the weighty matters being discussed.

Jolene's determination shone through as she expressed her confidence in taking on the task. She also recognised the hunger they all felt, suggesting they find a nice place to have dinner and discuss the details further. Jolene admitted that she hadn't eaten all day.

Maria quietly noted to herself Jolene's tendency to skip meals lately, understanding the challenge it posed. She resolved to keep a closer eye on Jolene, to prevent any potential eating disorders from developing, knowing how difficult it would be for her to do with the increased workload.

In response to Maria's concern, she asked about Jolene having her own personal driver to cover the extensive area she would now need to manage. Also, the other girls would need to be dropped off and picked up safely. Shady nodded in agreement, assuring Maria that they would assign trusted individuals to the task. Maria felt relieved but she still needed to discuss Jolene's eating habits with Shady, ensuring the new driver's role would also entail making sure that Jolene ate properly.

Shady interrupted Maria's thoughts, redirecting the conversation, to ask where they should go for dinner. The question prompted them to shift their focus away from work, giving them a much-needed distraction from the business.

CHAPTER 8: Requisition.

The following weeks were quite challenging for Jolene. She was rarely at home, as she was actively recruiting care home girls. Her recruitment efforts had taken her to various places like Warwickshire, Worcester, and even Stafford. Despite the demanding task, Jolene found an ally in her new driver, Tye. Their friendship was growing, Tye had been hired by Shady, who had a long-standing relationship with Tye's father. Shady believed that having a younger driver would allow Jolene to relate better to him. Tye was thrilled to be working with Jolene, who was not only mature for her age, but she made him feel like they had a deeper connection, although he acknowledged the age difference between them. One of Tye's responsibilities was to ensure that Jolene ate properly, so they often visited cafes together for meals. They enjoyed each other's company, Tye always supported Jolene whenever she needed him to, making her laugh and providing companionship. Aside from her recruitment efforts, they spent a significant amount of time together. Jolene and her team of girls were close to reaching their recruitment target, with only one care home left, with four days remaining before Otis returned home. Jolene had put in a tremendous effort with the assistance of her senior girls. The work was arduous and stifling, time with Tye was her only silver lining. He made her feel normal, he made her feel special, he made her laugh.

Maria had also been occupied with her own recruitment efforts, successfully bringing in thirteen more women to work for Otis on the streets. She felt a sense of satisfaction with her work, knowing that the majority of these women were desperate single mothers who had grown tired of struggling to make ends meet. Some of them had issues with drug use, with a few being regular marijuana users and two having a cocaine addiction to support. The rest of the women were simply driven by their desperate need for money. Maria's approach was relatively straightforward, she would frequent pubs in various council estates and strike up conversations with the women. The only downside was that a few of them battled with alcoholism, but considering their recruitment location, it wasn't entirely unexpected.

While Maria admired Jolene's dedication, she couldn't help but notice how exhausted she seemed these days. Although Maria also observed a noticeable spark in Jolene's demeanour whenever she was in the company of Tye. Tye was a decent young man, albeit older than Jolene, but he treated her well. Maria couldn't help but worry about the possibility of a romantic involvement between them, knowing how possessive Otis could be. It could cause no end of trouble.

Jolene anxiously waited for Tye to pick her up, knowing it was dinner time. She had successfully completed her recruitment drive two days prior, adding an impressive eighty-nine girls to their team. She acknowledged that the process had been challenging, and she couldn't afford to be as selective as she typically would have been. Some of the girls were already involved in soliciting in their respective areas, but Jolene enticed them with higher pay and the added security of indoor parties at well-guarded houses. It was a tempting offer for these young girls who recognized the dangers of working the streets. They eagerly accepted the opportunity to work for Jolene and Otis, knowing they would be protected.

Jolene felt a sense of dread as Otis's return drew near. She couldn't help but feel annoyed by the fact that Otis's recent trip to Trinidad apparently went smoothly, without any incidents or legal trouble. She pushed aside these thoughts as Tye arrived to pick her up for dinner.

Shady was extremely pleased with the girls' success in meeting their targets, particularly Jolene, who consistently amazed him. She possessed both intelligence and beauty, which made her a formidable combination despite her young age. However, Shady couldn't help but notice that Tye and Jolene had grown too close for comfort. While Shady genuinely liked Tye and recognized his value to the organization, he knew that if Otis caught wind of the affection between Tye and Jolene, he would obliterate the young man without a second thought. Shady realized he needed to have a serious conversation with Tye, perhaps even change his route, so that Tye would be driving the other girls instead. Deep down, Shady understood that this decision would upset Jolene, but he had to avoid being the one to inform Tye's father that his son had been murdered by Otis. Due to his territorial jealousy, Otis would eliminate Tye in an instant, without any hesitation. In Otis's twisted world, if he was lonely, then everyone else should be too. Not that Otis even comprehended love, for he was incapable of experiencing it.

As Tye sat in the driver's seat, he couldn't help but smile at Jolene. His captivating appearance stirred something deep within her. Tye was undeniably handsome, being with him made Jolene's days more bearable. She cherished their time together, finding comfort in his good-natured, gentle characteristics. Tye had a calming effect on her, and she could feel herself falling deeply for him. Despite knowing she shouldn't, Jolene couldn't deny that Tye embodied everything she desired in a man. He was a stark contrast to Otis. They had become inseparable, and Jolene cherished every single moment spent with him.

Likewise, Tye relished his time with Jolene. He sensed his feelings growing for her, but he refused to act on them due to her age. <u>He recognized</u> that she was too young for him, but he was willing to wait until her sixteenth birthday, it was only three years away. He held strong to his morals, refraining from making any sexual advances. Jolene meant everything to him, he couldn't imagine being with anyone else. From her silky blonde hair to her captivating blue eyes, he was certain that Jolene was his soulmate. Tye was determined to do right by her, he envisioned marrying her someday. For now, he would savour their time together, understanding that his father had always said he would <u>recognize</u> his soulmate when he found her, and Tye was convinced that Jolene was precisely that. His soulmate.

The following day, Shady arranged to meet with Tye at their office once he had finished driving Jolene around. Shady sat behind his desk, going through paperwork and bills, preparing for Otis's imminent return. The door opened, and Tye walked in, slightly concerned. "You asked to see me," he said.

Shady nodded and motioned for Tye to sit down. "Indeed, I did. Otis is arriving tomorrow, and as you know, he is Jolene's stepfather. Both Maria and I have noticed that you and Jolene have become quite close," Shady began. Tye was about to protest his innocence when Shady raised his hand, signalling for him to let him finish. "Now son, here's the thing. If Otis catches wind of your closeness to Jolene, he'll go ballistic. No one is allowed near his women, especially not his stepdaughter." Tye felt as if he had been punched in the gut, but he knew he had to listen. Shady's facial features said it all, this was a serious matter.

Shady continued, acknowledging Tye's character. "I know there's nothing sexual between you. You're a good lad, your father raised you right. But Otis won't see it that way. So, tomorrow will be your last day as Jolene's driver. You'll be in charge of running the East territory with the other girls. You must stay away from Jolene when Otis is around, or it could cost you your life. Do you understand what I'm telling you?" Tye was visibly shaken by the revelation. This meeting was not what he had expected at all. He had heard rumours about Otis's sadistic nature, but he never imagined it would be to this extent. In fact, Tye had secretly hoped that Otis would like him and accept him into the family, not just as a member of the firm. Inside, he felt a surge of anger, but he kept it hidden. The realisation of being separated from Jolene was hard to swallow. He was infatuated with her, but he also didn't want to end up dead.

Tye nodded silently, struggling to come to terms with the difficult situation he now faced.

"You're right, Jolene will be devastated," Tye expressed with a heavy heart. "Can I ask for your permission to tell her tomorrow over dinner? I believe she deserves a proper goodbye. It's the least I can do." Shady nodded in agreement, whilst taking into account that Otis's flight wasn't arriving until the early hours of the next day.

With that settled, Tye left the office and drove home as sadness enveloped him. He planned to discuss the situation with his father, seeking his advice and guidance. He decided that he would take Jolene somewhere special for their last meal together. Above all else, Tye wanted to ensure that Jolene understood his genuine feelings for her. He would wait for her no matter how long it took. His heart felt heavy, as if his world had been shattered. The thought of not being able to see her was overwhelming, but he resolved to find a way to cope with the upcoming separation. Whatever it took, he would find a way to be with her, he would save money for their future, he would watch her from afar. He knew Otis was dangerous, but one way or another he would be with his Jolene.

CHAPTER 9: Emptiness.

Jolene's mind was filled with confusion. When Tye had picked her up from the house, she sensed a noticeable change in his demeanour. He was unusually quiet and distant. He was acting strange, he looked sad and afraid. The impending return of Otis in the early hours added to her anxiety. Despite exceeding his targets, Jolene remained uncertain, about how Otis would react to her accomplishments. Her gut instinct warned her that darker times lay ahead. She couldn't shake the feeling that something terrible was about to happen, a foreboding that chilled her to the core.

Jolene had overheard Maria and Shady discussing the atrocities Otis had committed against the two brothers in Trinidad. The knowledge of his sadistic nature only served to validate Jolene's feelings about him. Otis was the devil incarnate, of that, she was sure. The thought of his potential actions weighed heavily on her mind. No matter what, she must stay focused and clear headed. Dismissing her troubling thoughts, she couldn't wait to meet Tye for dinner. He had become an essential presence in her life, filling a significant void. Being with him made all her troubles fade away. But earlier he was distant, and she didn't know why. For now, she had to get her head in the game, she must stop these thoughts. She needed a clear head.

The meeting with the new girls went smoothly, they were ready to start working that night. Tye would pick them up after they had dinner. The party would be held at one of their rented residential properties in the suburbs, a well-furnished three-bedroom flat situated above a takeaway on the bustling high street. Its inconspicuous location ensured minimal attention from the outside world. Once the clients and girls arrived, the party would be fuelled with alcohol and recreational drugs. Jolene planned to join them, intending to guide the new girls and help them feel comfortable in their new environment. Despite her role as a manager, she still engaged in seeing clients herself, although she admitted to despising it now.

Jolene couldn't shake the feeling of being unfaithful to Tye, even though they were not in a relationship. What troubled her more was the fact that Tye had never made any romantic advances towards her. At times she questioned if he even felt that way about her. Would he ever desire her? She believed that only time would reveal the truth of their relationship. Jolene and Tye found themselves having dinner at an exquisite Italian restaurant, a departure from their usual casual cafe outings. Tye had insisted on treating Jolene and paying the bill, which left her pleasantly surprised. Maybe he did like her that way, after all.

Curiosity got the better of her, and she couldn't help but ask, "Why are we here Tye? What's with the fancy dinner?"

Taking a sip of water, Tye gathered his courage before speaking. "Before I begin, Jolene, please know that I am deeply and completely in love with you," he confessed. Jolene's cheeks blushed slightly as she struggled to comprehend his words. Tye continued, "However, this will be our last shift together. Shady has moved me to the East team, and I don't know who will be driving you around starting tomorrow."

Jolene's heart sank as the reality sank in. "But why? Why would Shady do such a thing?" she whimpered, her voice filled with anguish.

Tye explained, "Apparently, everyone has noticed how close we've become, and Shady believes your stepfather would be furious if he discovered my feelings for you." A moment of heavy silence followed, and Tye spoke once more, his voice tinged with sadness. "You heard me correctly, I did say, I love you. But I also understand the immense temper of your stepfather. He believes he owns his women and daughters entirely. I will wait for you as long as it takes, but for now, we must follow Shady's orders. He's only looking out for us. We'll have to keep our distance, even though I don't want to. I also, don't want to risk my life." Tears streamed down Jolene's cheeks, and Tye gently wiped them away with his hand. "I love you too," she confessed, her voice filled with emotion. The food on their plates no longer held any appeal for them. Jolene vowed to speak with Maria, convinced that she could find a way for them to still see each other. Jolene couldn't bear the thought of being without Tye, he had become her everything, her life would be incomplete without him.

"MEMORIES"

'Even though Tye has professed his love for me, he still won't touch me. Why won't he touch me? All I want is to feel his lips on mine. If he loves me, why won't he kiss me? Everything is so confusing. To be perfectly frank, that hurts me. It's as though he doesn't want me. When we're together I am at my happiest, but I also worry that Otis will find out about us. I am terrified that he will hurt Tye. The only time I feel truly content is when I'm with Tye. I'm afraid he won't wait for me, that he doesn't really want me, because I am damaged goods. His eyes see into my soul. I adore him. I get butterflies in my tummy when I am with him. He says he'll wait until I am sixteen, and then we'll elope, but what about Alice? We have never talked about Alice. Is this all just a pipe dream? or is there some truth behind it? Does he really love me? like I love him. Will he really wait for me for three long years? He promised to be my hero, to take me away from this life. Or maybe it's all an elaborate delusion I've conjured up in my head, to distract myself from the truth. I love him so much it hurts. He can't possibly love me, I'm damaged goods.'

That night, Tye dropped Jolene off at the party flat. Jolene wasn't in the mood to work, but she knew she had no choice. It was essential for the new girls to see her in action, earning their trust and helping them feel more at home. As the party grew crowded with thirty men and the four young girls, Jolene began showing the girls how things worked. The doorman collected the money, and the girls would receive their share once the party was over, and the last client had left. Each girl engaged with the clients, taking their turns with the men. Throughout the night, Jolene couldn't stop thinking about Tye. He had professed his love for her, and she appreciated that he respected her age and wouldn't be intimate until it was legally allowed. He truly loved her, nobody had ever shown such care and understanding towards her age before. Tye was a good and decent man, and Jolene didn't want to let Otis keep them apart. Lying on the bed, watching the ceiling while engaging with a client, they could have her body, but her mind, her thoughts were hers alone. As she lay there with the client grunting in her ear, Jolene made a firm decision. She would find a way to see Tye behind Otis's back. Jolene believed she was clever enough to outmanoeuvre Otis in this situation, without giving any consequences a second thought.

Otis's plane was scheduled to land at 3 am, providing Jolene with a small window of time to talk with Maria after her work. Maria was already aware of the situation, having been informed by Shady the day before. While she sympathised with Jolene, Maria understood that it was in everyone's best interest to keep them apart. Otis would go as far as killing Tye if he found out about their relationship, and Maria feared that Jolene would suffer a severe beating as well. As Jolene returned home, before she could utter a word, Maria sternly interjected, "You cannot see each other anymore. That poor lad could lose his life over this, don't you understand?". Overwhelmed with emotions, Jolene burst into tears, exclaiming, "But we love each other."

Maria's anger began to escalate. *"If you truly love him, you wouldn't ask him to risk his life for you. I won't assist you in hiding this. you know better than anyone that there's no way to keep things from Otis. Not to mention the unimaginable consequences he would inflict upon you if he found out. You must end this now Jolene. Honestly, I don't know what's gotten into you lately. You're well aware of Otis's nature, it's just too dangerous."*

The conversation left Jolene devastated and conflicted, realizing the severity of the situation and the risks involved. She had to come to terms with the fact she could no longer see Tye, as painful as it was. The fear of Otis's wrath and the concern for Tye's safety outweighed their love, forcing Jolene to accept the heart-breaking reality. Jolene acknowledged that Maria's perspective made sense, but the thought of living without Tye was difficult to bear. At least for now, they needed to create some distance between themselves. Otis had a tendency to meddle in everything and seemed to have informants everywhere. Jolene would have to live in the hope, that only Shady and Maria had noticed the deepening connection between her and Tye. It might be for the best if they both kept a low profile and avoided each other until they could gauge Otis's behaviour on his return. Jolene believed that meeting Otis's demands would please him, she prayed it might grant them a respite from his cruelty as a form of compensation. Determined, she wiped away her tears and reassured Maria that she fully understood her concerns, she would never put Tye in jeopardy. Relieved, Maria hugged Jolene and expressed that for now, it was the only way to ensure Tye remained safe and out of Otis's clutches.

CHAPTER 10: New blood.

That night, Jolene made the decision to sleep in Alice's bed, a ritual she always followed when she felt worried or concerned about Alice's well-being. She wanted to make sure she was there for her sister, if Otis barged into their room in the middle of the night, she would shield her, or at least try too. Their bond was incredibly strong, even though Alice rarely spoke. Maria had gone to work in the red-light district, and Jolene, utterly exhausted from the day's events, couldn't bear the thought of waiting up for Otis. She hoped he wouldn't be angry with her in the morning. The anticipation of his return loomed over them all like a dark cloud, casting a shadow on their lives. When he was home, everyone walked on eggshells, afraid that a single misplaced word could trigger his rage. His cruelty affected everyone in his presence, Jolene feared what the upcoming months would bring. As she climbed into bed with Alice and nestled close to her, Alice unexpectedly spoke, "I'm scared too sis, but one day he will not be able to hurt us ever again." It sent shivers down Jolene's spine. Despite her unease, Jolene drew nearer to her little sister and whispered, "I love you, and I'll take care of us. One day, we'll be together, and this nightmare will fade away. You're right, little one, one day we'll be free." With those words, they both drifted off to sleep.

    The following morning, Alice and Jolene awoke to the sound of laughter emanating from the kitchen, a rare occurrence in their household. Clad in their nightdresses, they tiptoed down the stairs, enticed by the inviting aroma of bacon and eggs. To their surprise, Shady and Otis were sitting at the table with an unfamiliar woman, while Maria bustled around the stove. It turned out that the lady was Shady's sister, who had returned from Trinidad with Otis, to assist them during her three-month visa stay. She had a warm and vibrant personality, instantly winning Jolene's admiration. Jolene was taken aback, unsure why Otis had allowed this arrangement. Shady's sister, Sherry, introduced herself to Alice, who immediately embraced her with a hug. Just then, Otis spoke up, praising Shady for the idea. Highlighting how it would enable Maria and Jolene to work longer hours now that Alice was taken care of. Shady looked ashamed, he had not informed the women of the household of his intentions when suggesting his sister stayed for a while. He naively believed she would lighten their workload and offer them a break. Unfortunately, Otis had other plans. Sensing the tension, Maria intervened, inviting the girls to sit down so they could all enjoy breakfast together.

Despite her exhaustion from working throughout the night, Maria rallied herself to finish clearing the breakfast table, enlisting the help of Alice, Jolene and Sherry.

Otis had accompanied Shady to the office to review the accounts and check if the girls had met their quotas, leaving the women to collectively breathe a sigh of relief. Sherry was curious about the family business, she sought to learn everything she could. While Shady had warned her about Otis, he had not provided any further details. Maria requested Jolene prepare a bath for Alice, so they could have a discussion, before Maria finally retired to her makeshift pull-out bed in the lounge. Maria was feeling unusually worn out today, the previous night's work had taken a heavy toll on her. Her body seemed to ache from within, but she attributed it to the strain of excessive work and her age. At thirty-nine, Maria felt much older than her years. Everything seemed to hurt nowadays, even walking the streets or enduring hours of standing in the cold felt like torture, despite her previous fondness for such experiences. She couldn't quite fathom the reason for her declining health, but she pushed those intrusive thoughts aside, promising herself that if the symptoms persisted for a few more weeks, she would schedule a doctor's appointment. Interrupting her thoughts, Sherry voiced her concern, saying, "Are you alright, Doux Doux? You appear a bit under the weather, if you don't mind me saying so."

Maria responded to Sherry with a fond yet dismissive tone, "I haven't heard 'Doux Doux' in years, it means sweetheart if I recall correctly, am I right?" Sherry nodded, impressed that Maria knew her dialect. Maria reassured Sherry, "I'll be alright," just as they sat down at the table, brewing a pot of tea and engaging in a heartfelt conversation. Sherry was taken aback upon learning about Jolene's involvement in the family business. As far as Sherry was concerned, children should never be entangled in the criminal underworld, they should be off limits. Maria patiently explained the situation to Sherry, which led Sherry to develop a deep-seated hatred for Otis, although she wisely kept her feelings to herself. All she could do was try to create a nurturing environment at home for Maria and the two young girls now under her care. Though it seemed that Otis had different plans for Jolene. After Maria finished updating Sherry on everything, she took some pain relief and retired to bed, leaving Sherry to look after the two girls. Jolene had just finished bathing, leaving Alice to play for a while. Alice adored the water, which sparked an idea in Jolene's mind, perhaps it would be possible for Alice to go swimming. She wondered if they could go together if Otis would allow it. Neither of them knew how to swim, but Jolene wondered whether Sherry could take them, considering she would be looking after Alice for a while. Maybe Sherry could convince Otis to agree to the idea.

Jolene quickly got dressed and towel-dried her long platinum, blonde hair before heading down to the kitchen. As she entered, Sherry asked her to take a seat, wanting to understand Jolene better and see what kind of person she was. Sherry was still trying to process what Maria had told her, she was determined to find a way to improve the girls' lives. Jolene sat at the table as she reached out to pour herself a cup of tea. Sherry sat there quietly, taking in Jolene's beauty, before asking, "How can I make things better for you and your sister? Shady asked me to come and help you both, he has grown quite fond of you. I know your stepfather is a beast." Jolene was shocked as no one had ever spoken about her stepfather in such a way. In that moment, Jolene immediately felt a connection with Sherry. She realised that Alice, her sister, needed more of a normal childhood and it seemed like Sherry genuinely wanted to help them. Jolene thought about how grateful she was too Shady, for bringing this woman into their home, as she kissed Sherry on the cheek. Then she sat back down to finish her tea and said, "Both Alice and I have always wanted to learn how to swim." On hearing this, Sherry raised her teacup in the air and said, "Done! We can go in the morning, so that it doesn't interfere with your work for Otis."

Jolene and Sherry exchanged a knowing smile, silently acknowledging their agreement. Jolene studied the woman in front of her. Sherry had a curvy figure and gentle facial features. Being in her forties, she exuded a maternal aura. In that moment, Jolene blurted out, "Do you have kids?". Sherry was slightly shocked by the question but responded honestly, "my dear, God never blessed me with that gift." Jolene sensed a hint of sadness in Sherry's voice. Not wanting to pry further, she left the conversation there and went to retrieve Alice from the bath and prepare her for the day.

Meanwhile, in the kitchen, Sherry contemplated her future with the girls. She knew that Otis, was not someone she could trust. She had grown up with Otis and Shady, and during their childhood, they had become like family. Sherry reasoned that perhaps she could soften Otis a little, remind him of their shared past, and maybe even win his favour enough to allow her to continue looking after Jolene and Alice. The girls desperately needed a mother figure, and Sherry yearned to be one, for them. It seemed like a good solution, even though she knew Shady wouldn't be pleased with the situation. Quietly making up her mind, Sherry vowed to win over Otis and become a mother figure to the girls, no matter what the cost. She understood that Alice may have some challenges, but the two sisters had already found a place in her heart.

CHAPTER 11: Grieving.

The following months were filled with joy and happiness with Sherry's presence, but Jolene couldn't help but feel miserable without Tye. Sherry had grown close to the girls, particularly during their swimming trips. Surprisingly, Alice had turned out to be a natural swimmer, impressing Jolene. Alice not only learned to swim but also mastered underwater swimming, holding her breath for almost the entire length of the pool. This earned her the nickname "petite mermaid," which delighted Alice to no end. She never wanted to leave the pool, as it became her safe haven. Alice effortlessly learned various swimming strokes. On the other hand, Jolene struggled with swimming and could only manage to doggy paddle. Despite enjoying being in the pool, Jolene seemed to have difficulty with the water, unable to even float properly. It felt as though her legs were weighed down by lead.

Sherry thoroughly enjoyed spending time with the sisters, she had also noticed that Otis had developed a fondness for her, even if it was primarily due to her cooking. When Otis returned from Trinidad, he was pleased with the work Jolene and Maria had done, and mostly left everyone alone as he focused on expanding his control over drug and weapon territories. Sherry had a sneaking suspicion that Otis was on his best behaviour around her, although nobody seemed to understand why.

During a heartfelt conversation one night, Jolene shared everything with Sherry that happened between herself and Tye. The following morning, during their swimming session, Sherry secretly arranged for Jolene and Tye to meet up, giving Jolene an alibi. Jolene remained unaware of Sherry's plan, as Sherry wanted to uplift Jolene's spirits. However, Maria had become a cause for concern recently. Sherry had been urging Maria to see a doctor, but Maria stubbornly refused. Sherry grew increasingly worried as Maria had lost a significant amount of weight, she had also started waking up later in the day, and Sherry had even caught her taking pain medication excessively. The only silver lining was that Jolene hadn't noticed how sick Maria had become, since Jolene was working tirelessly all over Birmingham to keep Otis satisfied. Jolene already had so much on her plate; Sherry didn't want to worry her further.

Sherry and Alice enjoyed their swimming session, relieved that Otis was on route to Nottingham, which would mean they were safe for the time being. Meanwhile, inside Tye's car, Jolene and Tye reunited as if no time had passed. It was clear that their separation had not diminished their deep affection for each other. Tye was elated to be near Jolene again, his heart overflowing with love, but he maintained his resolve not to kiss her. He was determined to avoid anything that could be misconstrued as inappropriate until she reached the legal age. His love for Jolene was unwavering, and he was willing to wait patiently for her. Jolene, however, couldn't help but feel hurt and struggled to comprehend his decision. "But it's just a kiss," she protested. Tye felt a growing frustration, torn between his desire to kiss her and his commitment to doing what was right. He wanted their connection to be pure and lawful. The other men in Jolene's life meant nothing to him, they were despicable in his eyes. He envisioned a future where he would rescue Jolene from the clutches of Otis and heal the wounds inflicted upon her. Tye was determined to save her, already setting aside money for their future together.

As the brief encounter between Jolene and Tye came to an end, Tye drove Jolene back to the swimming baths in silence. Jolene couldn't quite grasp Tye's perspective. She couldn't understand why she was good enough for others but not for Tye. The thought never crossed her mind that Tye refused to be a paedophile. He refused to sink to depraved levels, even though he was unwittingly complicit in some of Otis's schemes. Both Jolene and Tye had gotten their hands dirty, but the difference was that Jolene was still a child while Tye was considered an adult. He recognised this distinction and couldn't comprehend why Jolene couldn't see it too. As he pulled up to where Sherry and Alice were waiting for Jolene's return, Tye reiterated his feelings once again, "I love you Jolene, but we have to wait. It has to be real and legal, or else I would never be able to live with myself. Please think about it and try to understand." With those words,

Jolene angrily slammed the car door and stormed off. Sherry was dumfounded by Jolene's reaction. She had expected the girl to be overjoyed. Instead, Jolene was visibly upset.

Sherry raised an eyebrow and inquired, "What happened? I thought you two would be thrilled to see each other again."

Jolene blurted out, "He won't kiss me! Why won't he kiss me?".

Sherry quickly realized that Jolene, despite her worldly knowledge, was still just a young teenager with much to learn. Sherry hugged Jolene, and Alice joined in, embracing them as much as her small arms would allow. Then, to everyone's surprise, Alice spoke up, saying, "He doesn't want to treat you like Otis does. Tye believes you deserve better. It's a good thing sis." Finally, Jolene understood. Sherry and Jolene exchanged a perplexed look. Alice, who rarely spoke, always seemed wise beyond her years. It was as if the young girl knew far more than most, despite being only ten years old, soon to be eleven. Alice was an enigma.

The three of them returned home to a quiet house, finding that Maria still hadn't woken up. Sherry felt a strange sensation pass through her body, as if something unsettling had occurred. Jolene expressed her desire to wake Maria, but Sherry suggested making tea first and taking a cup to Maria's room to wake her. Jolene agreed, she had been missing her interactions with Maria. Lately, it seemed as though they lived in separate worlds, their paths rarely crossing due to conflicting schedules. "Here you go, Jolene. Take this to her and wake her up. She'll appreciate a cup of tea in bed," Sherry said, handing Jolene the hot mug of tea. Jolene accepted it gratefully and entered Maria's room to wake her.

Suddenly, Sherry heard Jolene's piercing screams, sending chills down her spine. Sherry and Alice rushed into the room to find Jolene clutching Maria's lifeless body. Jolene's cries echoed, "No, no, no, don't leave me. Come back! Please come back."

Alice broke down in tears upon witnessing the heart-wrenching scene. Both girls were inconsolable. Sherry did her best to provide comfort, but her own heart weighed heavily with sorrow. Jolene refused to let go of Maria, holding her lifeless body tightly and rocking back and forth. Alice, exhausted from her emotions, huddled in a corner of the room, quietly sobbing. Neither of them wanted to leave Maria's side. Sherry called for an ambulance, her voice trembling with grief, whilst trying to understand the events that unfolded before her.

Once the ambulance arrived to take Maria's body, Sherry managed to calm both girls and provide them with sweet tea to help them cope with the shock. With a heavy heart, Sherry made the difficult call to inform Shady about Maria's sudden death. Shady was completely shocked by the news, as Maria's passing was unexpected and left everyone puzzled. They knew they would have to wait for the autopsy report to understand the cause. Sherry shared with Shady that Maria had been unwell for some time but had refused to seek medical help. Maria had taken the details of Lorna's death to her grave.

"MEMORIES"

'It was Marias death that brought back the visions of my mother's death, and now this whole house reeks of it. Reeks of death. Another person I love has died. Those who have passed haunt me. Although Maria and I had our differences, I eventually felt sad for her and stopped holding her responsible for my mother's death. Because I learned that she had no control over the situation either. She protected us and assisted me in creating a powerful business for Otis's benefit. Thanks to Maria's ingenuity, we managed to keep Alice safe. What kept her from visiting the doctor? How come I didn't realise she was sick? I'm to blame; I should have realised what was happening. When I found her that fateful morning, I was shocked to see how much weight she had lost. On her death bed, she was finally given her freedom. I was afraid I would crush her frail body as I hugged her so tightly, refusing to let go, the paramedics had to force me away. Why did she leave me, why? Why do they all have to die? Without her support, I have no idea how I will be able to keep Otis away from Alice. Maria was the brains and knew how this horrible society we live in functions. How are we going to make it without her? I beg you God, to stop taking the people I care about away from me.'

Sherry did her best to console the girls, who had already experienced so much loss in their young lives. First, their mother, and now Maria. Sherry made a firm decision to talk to Otis about allowing her to stay and care for the girls. The only obstacle was her visa, but she hoped that with Otis's connections, there might be a solution. Sherry had sent the girls to their room so that she could clean up the lounge, erasing any trace of the tragic event. The police had already conducted their investigations, and Sherry thought it was best to restore the room to its former use, although she knew that it might require repainting and a new sofa. They couldn't leave the sofa there, not after Maria had died on it. Shady had asked Otis to order a new sofa for the home. Sherry was determined to redecorate the room and have the sofa Maria had passed away on removed. She had never dwelled on death, as she had experienced her own father's passing when she was young. She had been the one to discover him slumped in his chair, having suffered a heart attack. Drawing from her own experiences, she believed she would be the best person to help the girls navigate through the grief of losing Maria.

CHAPTER 12: City lights.

Shady and Otis were still in Nottingham, having stopped for a late lunch at a pub to discuss business before their meeting with the Palmer crew. However, Shady found it difficult to concentrate on what Otis was saying. He couldn't shake off the sadness he felt over Maria's passing, even though he had to hide his true emotions from Otis. Shady wondered if Otis would take responsibility for Maria's funeral expenses, but deep down, he knew that Otis wouldn't care. It seemed as though Otis was indifferent to Maria's fate, despite her being his top recruiter until Jolene came into the picture. While they sat eating their meals, Otis casually mentioned, "The Palmer crew will be beneficial for us. They'll supply us with guns and drugs, and we can sell them at a higher price." Irritated by Otis's nonchalant attitude, Shady interjected, "Otis, Maria is dead, and you haven't said a word. Are you going to leave her with a pauper's funeral? Don't you care about your girls? They will be devastated." As soon as the words left his mouth, Shady regretted his outburst. He knew better than to confront Otis in such a way, as it would be seen as a challenge, and crossing Otis was dangerous. Shady quickly backtracked, saying, "Listen, I'll take care of her funeral arrangements. Nothing extravagant, just enough so the girls can say a proper goodbye. While you focus on dealing with the Palmers, let me handle this for you. I'll even pay for it but tell the girls it was all your doing. Does that sound fair?". Otis smirked sarcastically, replying, "Well, if you want to make me look good, that's great. It's what I pay you for, remember? You're here to make me appear less volatile and show that I have a heart. It's your job to conceal my true nature from everyone, including my girls." Shady nodded, relieved that he had managed to avoid a major conflict, but he scolded himself for even speaking out in the first place.

Shady and Otis ended up staying overnight in Nottingham as requested by the Palmer crew. The crew insisted that either Shady or Otis personally handle the upcoming shipment of goods back to Birmingham, which made Shady uneasy. Typically, they relied on drivers to handle such tasks, but the Palmer crew insisted on dealing directly with Shady or Otis. Otis was capable of driving, but he preferred to be chauffeured by Shady.

During their stay, the Palmer crew expressed interest in the care homes scheme and expressed their desire to expand their own operations based on Otis's successful business model. Of course, they offered Otis a cut of the profits, acknowledging that the idea originated from him. Otis kept the fact that the idea was actually Jolene's and Maria's a secret. He saw Jolene as his secret weapon, unsure of how the Palmer crew would handle recruitment without her. But that was not his concern. They would run their own business, and as long as they cut him in, he was satisfied. The Palmer crew arranged for Otis to receive a tidy ten percent of the profits. All he had to do was provide them with the business plans, and they would take care of the rest. Otis saw it as the beginning of a promising partnership.

Shady, on the other hand, had reservations. He was well aware of the Palmer crew's notorious reputation, as they didn't shy away from their criminal activities. Everywhere they went in Nottingham, they were treated like visiting royalty. Shady knew that their notoriety would eventually lead to their downfall, and he didn't want himself and Otis to be dragged down with them. He knew of the danger of being associated too closely with the Palmers.

That night, Otis and Shady joined the Palmer crew at one of their exclusive restaurants before heading to the Palmer club. The club was an impressive venue, featuring dancers in cages positioned throughout the space. Drinks flowed freely, and lines of white powder were available for those who wished to indulge. Otis declined, considering drugs to be a risky endeavour, but Shady, seeking consolation from his sorrows, eagerly partook in the drugs. Hoping that the haze of drugs and the lively atmosphere would temporarily alleviate his pain, Shady snorted a few lines.

The Palmers also provided women as hostesses, who sat with the men in the private room. Some of the women became overly friendly with the men, encouraged by the Palmer crew. Otis found himself with a girl kissing him on his lap, her hands exploring beneath his trousers, while Shady had two twin blondes nibbling on his neck. Despite the girls' youth, no older than twenty, Shady was too intoxicated and apathetic to care. It had been years since he had last been with a woman, and in his altered state, the allure of the moment overpowered his moral compass. At the end of the night, Otis and Shady brought the women back to their hotel room, continuing the party. Otis was pleased to see that his old friend still had the same vigour, having worried that Shady's sense of morality had compromised him in recent times.

Back at Otis's, Sherry found solace amidst the chaos of her life. With a resolute determination, she whisked the girls away to the cinema, leaving behind the burdens of their reality. Then after, Sherry enlisted Jolene and Alice, to embark on the mission to revitalise the front room. The walls, once adorned with faded memories, now awaited a fresh coat of paint to breathe new life into the space. The room stood before them, a hollow shell of its former self. Every trace of its previous inhabitants had been erased, leaving nothing but an empty canvas awaiting a fresh stroke of life. Sherry, the mastermind behind this transformation, had graciously given the girls the power to decide the room's new colour scheme. The impending arrival of the new Sofas, creating a sense of urgency over the task at hand. Time was of the essence, for the painting had to be completed without delay. Sherry's heart fluttered with excitement as she gazed upon the exquisite floor tiles before her.

They possessed a remarkable resemblance to the rich, luxurious allure of wooden flooring. Her passion for interior design ignited a fire within her, compelling her to acquire these tiles for this project. The girls had chosen materials with shimmering golds and regal Caribbean blues, much to Sherry's delight. The vibrant hues evoked a sense of nostalgia, transporting her back to the familiar comforts of her homeland. The room exuded an air of opulence, its walls adorned with a captivating wallpaper that served as a striking focal point. The chosen design, a daring departure from the ordinary, commanded attention and whispered secrets to those who dared to listen. The remaining walls, bathed in a soft shade of magnolia, provided a delicate balance of light and darkness, a subtle interplay that heightened the room's allure. As the girls embarked on their task of decorating the room, Sherry selected a local radio channel to accompany their endeavours, allowing the room to be filled with singing from the girls. They all remained deeply troubled by the loss of Maria, their hearts heavy with sorrow. Yet, amidst the darkness that enveloped them, Sherry emerged as a beacon of light, determined to guide them through the treacherous labyrinth of their anguish. She spared no effort in her quest to mend their shattered spirits, offering a compassionate hand to lift them from the depths of their grief.

Jolene's heart skipped a beat as Tye materialised at the door, Sherry had orchestrated a rendezvous for Tye and Jolene, in Otis's absence. As Tye stood there on her doorstep his unexpected presence sent a shiver down her spine. She swiftly regained her composure, masking her initial surprise with a facade of calm. A flicker of excitement ignited within her, for his arrival brought with it a glimmer of hope and the promise of assistance. And, perhaps, a chance to bask in his attention once more. It happened to be his day off, affording him the opportunity to lend a hand in their venture to clear out the lounge. Not only did he graciously offer his assistance in relocating the sofa Maria had passed away on, but he also gallantly volunteered to adorn the focal wall with a fresh layer of wallpaper. Tye's knowledge of Maria was limited, yet he understood the significance she held in Jolene's life. Despite the inherent risks associated with being within the confines of the family home and in such proximity to Jolene, Tye's determination to rectify matters for her was unwavering. If nothing else, he could do this for her and be here for her for these precious few hours.

In fleeting instances such as these, they relished the chance to be in each other's company. Sherry found herself captivated by the undeniable bond shared between Tye and Jolene, as if their souls were intricately woven together by fate itself. Her admiration for Tye's morals knew no bounds. He possessed an enigmatic allure that set him apart from the rest, in their dark and treacherous world. Every corner of the living room was now adorned with meticulous craftsmanship. Intricate patterns enhanced the walls, their delicate brushstrokes telling a story of elegance and refinement. The collective efforts of the group were nothing short of remarkable, everyone, pouring their heart and soul into the task at hand. Alice had gone above and beyond; crafting cushion covers and curtains that perfectly complemented the feature wall. As the golden yellow sofas were delivered, their arrival marked the final piece of elegance required to complete the project.

Shady's voice crackled through the phone, a whisper of urgency in his words. He informed them that he and Otis were en route from Nottingham, their return delayed by an unforeseen circumstance. A stealthy operation had forced them to unload their precious cargo from their vehicle, an action that demanded both time and discretion. Tye swiftly departed the premises the moment the call had arrived, his instincts urging him to avoid any chance of discovery within the confines of the house. Jolene's heart swelled with gratitude towards Sherry, the architect behind their rendezvous. In the shadows of their brief encounters, a dangerous dance of secrecy unfolded, binding them together. Jolene's heart fluttered with a newfound sense of freedom; her burdens momentarily lifted by the wonderful day she had shared with Tye.

Beneath the surface of her elation, an undercurrent of unease persisted. The weight of the world seemed to rest upon her shoulders as she pondered the daunting task that lay ahead. Maria, her trusted confidante, and mentor, had left her, leaving her to navigate the dark criminal underworld, of the business all on her own. The future of the enterprise hung in the balance, and she couldn't help but wonder if she possessed the strength and cunning necessary to steer the ship. Maria, with her extensive network and abundant resources, was the linchpin of their operation. Without her, Jolene feared they would be left bereft, lacking a crucial component of their illicit enterprise. Maria had been shrewd and meticulous, in her role of bookkeeper. With unwavering determination, she ensured that the figures aligned flawlessly, leaving no room for error. Her keen eye scrutinised every transaction, skillfully minimising any unnecessary expenses that dared to cross her path.

As Sherry savoured her dinner, her keen eyes caught a glimpse of Jolene, the girl was lost in the labyrinth of her own contemplations. Jolene's countenance betrayed a sense of detachment, her eyes fixed on some distant horizon. The air between them grew heavy with unspoken words, as if a veil of secrecy had descended upon their conversation. "What troubles you, Jolene?" Sherry inquired. Jolene's voice trembled as she responded, her eyes darting nervously around the warmth of the kitchen. "I'm lost, Maria possessed an arsenal of knowledge, an intricate web of contacts, and she was the mastermind behind our financial affairs," she confessed, her words laced with a hint of desperation. Sherry, responded, "I can balance the books for you. I have always harboured a passion for numbers." In that pivotal moment, a mischievous glimmer danced in Jolene's eyes, her lips curling into a triumphant grin. Sherry had unknowingly thrown her a lifeline, a chance to turn the tides in her favour, once again.

Mathematics was never Jolene's forte, a fact that could be traced back to her premature departure from education. As the thought funnelled its way into the depths of her mind, a glimmer of curiosity sparked within her. "Sherry," she uttered, her voice laced with a hint of intrigue, " Would you teach me? To balance the books." Sherry extended her arms, inviting Jolene into an embrace. The young girl eagerly rushed into Sherry's waiting arms, seeking the warmth of her presence. In a hushed tone, Sherry murmured, "Fear not my child, of course I will teach you."

CHAPTER 13: Inflicted wounds.

The night had grown darker, the moon casting an eerie glow upon the deserted streets. As they approached the house, a flickering light emanated from within, revealing the silhouette of a woman standing by the entrance. Sherry had been anxiously awaiting their return. Her eyes, sharp as a hawk's, pierced through the darkness, searching for any signs of the two men. Her heart raced as she awaited Otis's approval of the newly decorated lounge. The now well-lit room, adorned with plush velvet curtains and ornate lamps, exuded an air of sophistication. Every detail had been meticulously crafted. She understood his temper would ignite if he suspected the exorbitant expenses involved, so she had ensured that every aspect of the operation remained economically viable.

The question lingered on her lips. Would he let her take over the book-keeping? The weight of the task at hand was not lost on her, she understood the significance it held for Jolene. The books held secrets that she was not yet privy too, they were a key to unlocking the mysteries that plagued their lives. And now, she stood on the precipice, ready to step into Maria's shoes and take on this perilous endeavour. Having lovingly, tucked the sisters into their beds, she proceeded to phone the doormen, all the while skillfully accounting for Jolene's conspicuous absence. Jolene was in no fit state to work tonight, she was exhausted and still grieving.

The air was thick with tension as she contemplated what she was about to do. Sherry had recognised the exhaustion etched on Jolene's face. It was a respite she desperately needed, if only for tonight. Shady and Otis strode into the house to be greeted by Sherry. With a subtle gesture, she beckoned them to follow, leading them into the front room. Otis, with a mixture of awe and curiosity, couldn't help but inquire, "how much did this intriguing assortment set me back?" Sherry swiftly interjected, her voice cutting through the tense air like a knife. She wasted no time in elucidating that the expenses were solely attributed to the selected paint, wallpaper, and sofas. Shady's lips curled into a grin as he locked eyes with Otis, his voice dripping with calculated charm. "Well Otis," he exclaimed, expertly playing to the man's inflated ego, "this place is now fit for a King."

" This deserves a celebration, does it not." Otis, purred. He resolved to retrieve his cherished bottle of rum, that had witnessed countless triumphs and defeats, to commemorate this auspicious occasion with all those present. Seated at the kitchen table, Sherry's heart raced with anticipation. The moment had arrived, to discuss the books, ripe with opportunity and fraught with risk, summoning every ounce of courage within her, she steeled herself ready to broach the subject with him. It was a make-or-break moment, a pivotal juncture in her life. "Otis," she purred, her voice dripping with intrigue, "may I ask you about something? It has come to my attention that you find yourself one man short now, with no one to balance the books. I find myself wondering if I might step in and pick up where Maria left off?" Shady's countenance betrayed a deep sense of unease, his mind consumed by the fervent desire to shield his sister from the treacherous world of their illicit affairs.

Little did he realise; he had failed to consider the inevitable void that would be left in Maria's absence. Otis flashed one of his signature winning smiles, his eyes gleaming with a mix of charm and cunning. "That sounds good to me. I do need an extra set of eyes and it's always good to keep it in the family."

"Excellent," Sherry replied, her voice laced with triumph as she revelled in the knowledge that she had successfully swayed Otis to her side. Their glasses clinked together in celebration.

Shady concealed his discontent with practised finesse. Sometime soon he would have to confront his sister and warn her of the dangers. Explaining how his sister was dancing with danger, her every move a calculated risk. The stakes were high, and he knew it. With each step she took, she delved deeper into the duplicitous world she had willingly entered. It was a game, a game where the consequences were dire. Otis possessed an unyielding spirit that brooked no coercion. To him, any attempt to manipulate or force his hand was an affront, a direct assault on his pride and autonomy. Shrouded in a cloud of suspicion, Shady was acutely aware of Otis's undeniable weakness for his sister. Yet, a lingering doubt gnawed at his core, a nagging uncertainty that prevented him from fully placing his faith in Otis's intentions towards her. In the dark underbelly of his existence, he revelled in the pain he inflicted upon the women who dared to cross his path. It was a twisted dance, a macabre symphony of suffering that seemed to follow him wherever he went. And now, as fate would have it, she had unwittingly stumbled into his malevolent favour. There was an air of inevitability about it all, as if the universe had conspired to bring them together. For he was a predator, a wolf in sheep's clothing, and she, a vulnerable lamb, unaware of the danger lurking in the shadows.

In the realm of their existence, a sense of tranquilly enveloped the inhabitants. Otis, a man of questionable character, found himself compelled to exhibit his most virtuous demeanour in the presence of Sherry. This peculiar transformation both delighted and bewildered Shady and Jolene, two individuals well-acquainted with the darker shades of his nature. In the depths of her heart, concealed beneath a veil of secrecy, Sherry had a secret desire. A flicker of hope within her, whispering the possibility that Otis, the enigmatic figure who had entered her life, was succumbing to the intoxicating embrace of love. He had resolved her Visa predicament, for she had seamlessly integrated into the fabric of their family. Otis, with an air of reluctance, appeared to harbour an unspoken desire to prevent her return to the distant shores of Trinidad.

Jolene, with a determined glint in her eyes, had been working relentlessly, striving to appease Otis. The parties were going well, and life seemed to be heading in the right direction for everyone.

Meanwhile, Alice, had once again started on the path of home learning. Shady had engaged in a heated exchange with his sister, but his impassioned words were met with an impenetrable wall of indifference. Shady, with his keen perception, had discerned Sherry's deep yearning for a sense of belonging, a desire to embrace a family she could truly claim as her own. However, it had become increasingly evident to Shady that Sherry was not prepared to relinquish her newfound existence alongside them, without a fierce struggle. Shady found himself taken aback by the depth of his sister's affection for the girls. It was a love that knew no bounds, consuming her entirely. In this new foreign land, his sister had firmly established her position in the family unit, from which she refused to be swayed. No one possessed the power to alter the resolute determination that had taken root within her. Otis had been exhibiting peculiar behaviour of late, granting Sherry unrestricted access to his household and entrusting her with the care of his daughters. It was as if he had a genuine appreciation for her presence in his life. Shady's mind was consumed by a lingering worry, a seed of doubt that had taken root deep within his consciousness.

The thought of Otis, that cunning figure, attempting to ensnare his sister in a web of romantic entanglement sent shivers down his spine. It was a dangerous game, one that Shady knew all too well. He had witnessed Otis's charm and charisma first hand, witnessed the way he effortlessly manipulated those around him. But his sister, she was different. She possessed a spirit that was untamed, a fire that burned brightly within her. She was not the type that Otis typically pursued, and yet, Shady couldn't shake the feeling that danger lurked just beyond the shadows. He couldn't deny his intuition, he sensed a dark aura permeating the surroundings, a foreboding presence. The weight of this realisation bore heavily upon him, for he understood all too well the dire consequences that would befall him should any harm befall his beloved sister. The thought of incurring their mother's eternal wrath was an unbearable burden he dared not shoulder.

Otis felt an overwhelming surge of elation as the partnership with the Palmers continued to line his pockets with a substantial amount of money. Jolene remained steadfast in her commitment to expand the care home enterprise well beyond the limitations set by Otis. Her desires always led her to venture into unfamiliar territories, seeking fresh prey to sustain his thriving enterprise that extended its reach as far as Wales and the Southwest. The autopsy report on Maria had finally arrived, revealing a chilling truth. It appeared that her demise was not due to a sudden act of violence, but rather a silent and insidious killer that had infiltrated her body. It was Cancer that had claimed her life, its merciless grip leaving her riddled with its destructive presence. At long last, the coroner had rendered his verdict, allowing for the orchestration of Maria's sombre funeral proceedings. Shady, true to his word, had assumed the responsibility.

Deep within the recesses of Otis's psyche, a sinister desire simmered, fuelled by the wounds inflicted upon his fragile ego. Just as darkness threatened to consume him, Sherry, had entered their lives, altering the course of Otis's twisted intentions. For the time being, his nefarious plans were reluctantly consigned to the depths of his consciousness, relegated to the back burner of his malevolent mind. In the corners of Otis's troubled existence, there existed a flicker of nostalgia, a cherished connection from his childhood. Sherry was a beacon of light amidst the darkness, she had been the sole source of goodness in his tumultuous life. So, when Shady, extended an invitation for her to grace him with her presence, Otis found himself grappling with disbelief.

Fortune had smiled upon her, bestowing a stroke of luck that would prove to be instrumental in the unfolding events. With her unparalleled skill in the delicate art of balancing the books, she had seamlessly assumed control over the intricate workings of the numerous teams within their firm. In the depths of his contemplation, a fleeting notion crossed his mind, a tantalising question of whether an encounter with Sherry would offer a respite from the desolation that had consumed him. Could she, in some inexplicable manner, reignite the flickering embers of his humanity? Yet, as swiftly as the thought materialised, he ruthlessly banished it from his consciousness. She possessed a value that far exceeded his initial estimations, a worth that extended beyond his wildest imagination.

"MEMORIES"

'No one from Maria's family came to her funeral. That's just so sad. Otis didn't make any effort to pay his respects either. Me and Alice had the support of Shady, Sherry, and Tye. This time around, I'm quite sure we both shed a river of tears. Should I feel bad that at Maria's burial, I shed more tears than at my own mother's? Sadness and heartache engulfed me. Women who worked in the same area as Maria in the red-light district came to pay their respects. Some of my friends even managed to miss class to be there. It seems funerals really do show peoples true colours. When I cried for Maria, I guess a part of me was also crying for my mother. I tried to hold back the tears, but they just kept coming. Tye did his best to reassure me, but he had to keep his distance in case Otis had spies watching us. I can't take any more deaths. Why do we have to go through so much heartache. Poor Alice was in so much distress, that her tiny body was trembling. That day, I am sure a part of us died too.'

CHAPTER 14: Torture.

Sherry had seamlessly woven herself into the intricate fabric of the business, deftly assuming the mantle once held by Maria. Deep within her, a seething resentment festered, fuelled by her disdain for the sordid nature of the enterprise. The involvement of young girls gnawed at her conscience. And the plight of poor Jolene, forced to cater to clients as well, only intensified her abhorrence. However, she was acutely aware that engaging in a futile struggle with Otis regarding this matter would yield no favourable outcome. This aspect of their operation was a veritable goldmine, indispensable for appeasing the insatiable Otis and funding their extravagant lifestyle.

Without it, their grandiose expenditures would crumble like a house of cards. In a gesture of gratitude, Otis had bought Sherry a gleaming, brand-new car. His chivalrous demeanour towards her, in turn, granted Alice and Jolene a newfound sense of liberation, a freedom they had long yearned for, but had been denied until now. In an artful display of persuasion, Sherry had successfully convinced Otis to give the girls a generous monthly bonus. This tantalising incentive was directly tied to their ability to cater to an increasing number of clients. It was a method that ensured the unwavering loyalty of the girls. Sherry trembled involuntarily as the chilling notion of Otis uncovering the forbidden relationship between Jolene and Tye infiltrated her mind.

She continued to orchestrate their rendezvous, nurturing their connection, despite the cautionary words of her brother, Shady. He had forewarned her of the perilous game she was playing, one that jeopardized not only their own lives, but the lives of all involved.

In the gritty streets of Nottingham, a dangerous alliance had formed. Their nefarious activities had entangled them with the notorious Palmer gang, as they worked tirelessly to expand their illicit shipment empire. As the moon cast its pale glow upon the dimly lit alley, Otis found himself torn between duty and desire, his thoughts complicating the task at hand. He knew that leaving Sherry to oversee his girls in his absence was a risky move, but the allure of the Palmer gang's notoriety, with the guns and drugs made it impossible to stay away. He wanted to learn all he could about their business dealings with the intention of taking it all for himself one day. Little did he know that this decision would set in motion a chain of events that would forever alter the course of their lives.

In an instant, a thunderous explosion shattered the air, unleashing a hailstorm of deadly projectiles. Otis and Shady found themselves thrust into a deadly dance with death, as the relentless barrage of bullets sought to claim their lives. Little did they know, their seemingly innocuous task of procuring a shipment would soon plunge them into the treacherous depths of gang warfare. Oblivious to the lurking danger, they remained blissfully unaware of the rival gang's nefarious plot to abscond with their coveted arsenal. Shady, stealthily extended his hand towards the recesses of the vehicle's interior. His fingers sought out the cool touch of his most prized possession - the Desert Eagle. A weapon of immense power and lethal precision, it had become an extension of his very being. The decision to stow the firearm within the glove compartment of the car's limited space had been a practical one. Shady's imposing physique, a testament to his formidable presence, left little room for frivolities.

As his hand closed around the familiar grip, Shady's mind raced with the possibilities that lay ahead. With the Desert Eagle now in his possession, he felt an undeniable surge of confidence coursing through his veins. It was a weapon that had seen him through countless trials, a steadfast companion in the face of adversity. Little did Shady know, however, that the events about to unfold would test the limits of his resolve. In this world of deceit and betrayal, where loyalties were as fickle as the wind, he would soon discover that his trusted Desert Eagle might not be enough to safeguard his very existence.

A bullet, propelled by an unseen force, tore through the fragile barrier of glass, finding its mark with unerring precision. Its deadly trajectory found its way in the vulnerable flesh of his shoulder, inflicting a searing pain that coursed through his body. With a swift and calculated movement, Otis extended his arm towards the glovebox, his fingers gripping the handle of his weapon of choice. In a moment of urgency, Otis's voice pierced through the chaos, commanding Shady to take immediate action. "Put your foot down," he bellowed, his words laced with a sense of urgency. Despite the pain from the blow he had just received, Shady wasted no time in obeying the order. There was no need for a second request, he understood the gravity of the situation all too well. In the dimly lit roads, their hearts raced, their very survival hanging in the balance, with no thought for the shipment they had to leave behind.

With a screech of wheels and a cloud of smoke, they accelerated towards the illustrious Palmers club. Their hearts pounded. Otis seethed with an indomitable fury, his eyes ablaze with a smouldering rage. Shady, his best friend and ally, now sat before him, blood cascading from a grievous wound on his shoulder. The crimson liquid stained his pressed white shirt. As they arrived at the dimly lit club, their footsteps muffled by the pulsating bass of the music, their eyes met with a shared determination. Without hesitation, they navigated through the crowd, their gazes fixed on the offices concealed at the rear of the establishment. The formidable security guards, their stern expressions etched with a hint of apprehension, reluctantly granted them passage into the inner sanctum. Shady, sank wearily into the plush embrace of a leather chair. Meanwhile, Otis, his nerves frayed and his temper ablaze, opted to remain on his feet, his restless energy manifesting in his agitated stance, a silent testament to the tumultuous events that had unfolded throughout the evening. Micky Palmer reclined in his leather chair; his piercing gaze fixed upon the two men before him. The room was heavy with tension, the air thick with anticipation.

With a casual flick of his wrist, he gestured for them to take a seat. "What's happened, gentlemen?" Micky's voice was smooth, betraying none of the curiosity that burned within him. His eyes darted from one man to the other, searching for any hint of deception. The room seemed to hold its breath, waiting for the truth to be unveiled. Otis seethed with fury, his eyes ablaze with a dangerous intensity. "In the midst of our anxious anticipation for the long-awaited shipment, chaos erupted. Shady, has been shot. And to add insult to injury, our coveted consignment vanished into thin air, leaving us empty-handed and feeling betrayed.

Tell me, did you orchestrate this sinister plot against us?" Micky Palmer, a man shrouded in an enigmatic aura, remained unmoved by the weighty accusations hurled by Otis. Rising from his seat, he towered over Otis, his loyal guards brandishing their firearms, ready to strike fear into the heart of their target. "Pay heed, Otis," he growled, his voice dripping with menace, as the two figures faced each other, their eyes locked in a tense exchange. The words hung heavy in the air, dripping with suspicion and veiled threats. "We don't arrange such affairs for our business associates," the first figure spoke, his voice laced with a hint of menace. "Rest assured, you won't be indebted to us for this particular shipment, that is, unless I uncover the unsettling truth that it was you who orchestrated its theft."

"Trouble has befallen us. A nefarious gang, their intentions as dark as the night, sought to pilfer the fruits of our labour for their own sinister gains." His voice, tinged with a subtle menace, escaped his lips. In a sudden twist of fate, Otis's seething rage dissipated as swiftly as it had materialised, leaving him in a state of eerie calm. The guards, sensing the shift in his demeanour, cautiously returned their firearms to their holsters, their fingers no longer poised on the triggers. As Otis lowered himself onto the worn-out armchair, his eyes locked onto the figure standing before him. With a voice laced with a mixture of frustration and desperation, he uttered the words that had been haunting his mind, "Why, oh why, did you not see fit to warn me?" Micky, with a glint of defiance in his eyes, justified his actions with a voice as smooth as silk. "Consider this," he began, his words hanging in the air like a thick fog. "Would you, my dear friend, be inclined to engage in any form of business with an establishment that finds itself embroiled in an unrelenting war?" His question, laced with intrigue, lingered, leaving his audience pondering the consequences of such an association.

Micky wasted no time, swiftly reaching for his phone to make a series of crucial calls. The first was to his trusted personal physician, a discreet and skilled practitioner who possessed the necessary expertise to extract the bullet lodged in Shady's flesh, to expertly stitch him back together. The second call was of a different nature, one that summoned his loyal brothers and sons to embark on a relentless pursuit. They were to unleash their wrath upon Nottingham, leaving no stone unturned until the perpetrators responsible for the harrowing events of this fateful night were brought to their knees.

CHAPTER 15 Inevitable.

Jolene found herself immersed in the valleys of South Wales for an entire week, diligently attending to the intricate details of acquiring fresh party properties. Accompanying her on this venture was none other than Tye, the trusted confidant who had once again been granted the privilege of chauffeuring Jolene at the request of Sherry. The couple, reunited at last, revelled in the intoxicating bliss of their togetherness. Each passing moment, like a stolen gem, was savoured with an insatiable hunger. Tye remained resolute in his conviction that he and Jolene were destined to remain mere acquaintances, despite the palpable undercurrent of desire that coursed through their every interaction. Only two and a half years remained, ticking away like the hands of a relentless clock, until the fateful day of Jolene's sixteenth birthday. With bated breath, he ticked each passing day off in his calendar, a tangible testament to his mounting anticipation.

In the bustling world of the Palmer Firm, Otis had become consumed by his work, leaving little time for anything else. This created the perfect illusion, a deceptive tranquillity that lulled everyone into a false sense of security. They believed that Otis, preoccupied as he was, would remain oblivious to their relationship. Indeed, one could not deny the transformation that had befallen Otis ever since Sherry had entered his life. Yet, beneath this veneer of change, lurked a malevolence that would inevitably rear its ugly head. Such was the pattern of his true character. Jolene found herself entangled in a web of intrigue as she prepared for the night's party. Four unfamiliar faces, fresh to the scene, stood outside the party house awaiting her arrival.

Their youth was striking. They looked so young, so small. As if they had been plucked from the very heart of the coalmines in Wales itself. In comparison to their counterparts, they appeared petite, almost fragile in stature. Jolene couldn't help but ponder if their slightness was a consequence of their lineage, generations toiling away in the unforgiving tunnels of the coalmines. Tye skillfully navigated the winding streets, finally arriving at the venue for the party house precisely at 7pm. He watched as Jolene gracefully exited the vehicle, her demeanour exuding an air of self-assuredness. It was evident that this had become second nature to her. In no time at all, the quartet of young girls, along with Jolene, found themselves immersed in a whirlwind of revelry, alongside their clients.

    However, amidst the mirth and merriment, an unsettling sensation began to gnaw at Jolene's core. In the sombrely lit room, amidst the haze of cigarette smoke, there sat a client whose unruly demeanour sent shivers down her spine. His boisterous nature and unsettling presence caused her hair to bristle, as if sensing the impending danger that lurked within his very being. Jolene found herself at the mercy of a man who exuded an air of danger and intrigue. With a voice that dripped with a sinister charm, he insisted that she accompany him throughout the night, promising a generous compensation for her time. His gaze, fixated solely on her, hinted at a hidden agenda lurking beneath his enticing proposition. With his offer, she would only have to be intimate with him, just the one client tonight, he had promised to make it worth her while. With a nod of acquiescence, she consented, her decision hinging upon the presence of a sufficient number of young women at the soirée, entrusted with the task of attending to the desires and demands of the remaining clients. Disregarding her nagging apprehensions, she succumbed to his persuasive charm and followed him into the bedroom. He extended his hand, offering her a tantalising concoction. Little did she know, that seemingly innocent drink would become the catalyst for a chain of events that would forever alter the course of her life. As the liquid touched her lips, a sinister haze descended upon her consciousness, enveloping her into oblivion. The world faded away.

    Tye stood in the shadows; his eyes fixed on the house before him. The moonlight cast a strange glow on the deserted street, amplifying his growing unease. Jolene was late, far later than usual. A sense of foreboding settled over him, tightening his chest with each passing minute. Time seemed to stretch, each tick of the clock echoing in his ears, as he anxiously awaited her arrival. Something wasn't right, and Tye's instincts told him that danger was afoot. Approaching the formidable figure of the doorman, he inquired about the whereabouts of the elusive Jolene. Oblivious to the passage of time, the doorman found himself embroiled in a heated exchange with his estranged wife over the telephone. Tye's heart quickened its pace, a foreboding sense of unease settling upon him like a thick fog. Deep within the recesses of his mind, a nagging intuition whispered of impending danger. Tye's eyes darted nervously, scanning his surroundings. A cold shiver ran down his spine.

Tye burst through the door of the house, with a commanding tone, he barked at the doorman to trail behind him, his heart pounding with a sense of urgency. Determined, he directed the doorman to meticulously scour each room. The air hung heavy with a thick haze of smoke, swirling, and curling around the room like a sinister spectre. The acrid scent of cheap aftershave permeated every corner, mingling with the tobacco fumes to create an assault on the senses. Two young girls, their eyes gleaming with mischief, sauntered through the crowd, their laughter like a siren's call. They weaved between the furnishings, their slender figures accentuated by the flickering candlelight.

The men, captivated by the girls' allure, were ensnared in their web of seduction. Like unsuspecting prey, they fell victim to their charms, their gazes locked on the tantalising duo. Whispers of anticipation and desire echoed through the room. Tye's footsteps echoed through the dimly lit hallway, the weight of his apprehension settling heavily upon his chest. With each passing moment, his heart sank deeper into the abyss of despair. As he made his way towards the bedrooms, a sense of impending doom hung in the air, suffocating his every breath.

The secrets concealed within these walls would soon unravel. With a sudden surge of determination, he forcefully pushed open the door, revealing a scene that sent shivers down his spine. Standing before him was a delicate, petite brunette girl, her presence juxtaposed against the backdrop of four towering, menacing figures. The sight alone was enough to churn his stomach, a sickening feeling that penetrated to the very core of his being. He burst through the door of the next bedroom, his heart pounding in his chest. The room was shrouded in darkness, the only source of light, coming from the dim glow of the moon filtering through the curtains.

As his eyes adjusted to the gloom, he caught sight of a figure in a crumpled heap on the bed. It was Jolene, her once vibrant blonde hair now dishevelled and tangled. In that fateful instant, terror consumed him. His heart, once a steady rhythm of life, now shattered into countless fragments, as if a malevolent force had torn it apart. He sprinted across the dimly lit room, approaching her disfigured countenance and bruised form. With every desperate step, he silently pleaded for a glimmer of life to remain within her shattered frame.

With bated breath, he delicately pressed his fingers against her wrist, searching for the tell-tale signs of life. The room was cloaked in an eerie silence, broken only by the faint ticking of an old grandfather clock. Time seemed to stand still as he awaited the verdict. And then, a glimmer of hope emerged. A faint but steady rhythm coursed beneath his touch, a testament to her resilience. Jolene lay motionless, her body a canvas of violence. Bruises adorned her delicate features, evidence of a merciless assault.

The room, now bore witness to the sinister act that had left her unconscious and broken. With a tenderness that belied his rugged exterior, Tye scooped her delicate form from the dishevelled bed. A soft, worn blanket enveloped her fragile frame, shielding her from the harshness of the world as he whisked her away to the waiting vehicle. As he made his exit, his commanding voice echoed through the room, issuing a stern decree that the festivities come to an abrupt halt. With a stern gaze, he approached the doorman, his eyes scanning the establishment.

The doorman, a burly figure, that was supposed to look after the girls, looked shamefaced. With menace in his eyes, Tye, leaned in closer, his voice low and commanding. "I want every single name," he declared, his words laced with an air of authority, "every single client name on the list, do you hear me?" Tye's heart burned with a relentless desire for vengeance, his immediate concern was to ensure Jolene would pull through what had befallen her. He yearned to see her safely nestled in the comfort of her own home, her dishevelled appearance restored to its former glory, and her weary body finally finding solace within the confines of her bed. The perpetrator responsible for inflicting such harm upon Jolene would soon face the consequences of their actions, as the events of this fateful night unfolded. In that very moment, Tye made a solemn vow to collaborate closely with Otis on this endeavour. In that fateful moment, a chilling indifference consumed him, heedless of the sinister consequences that lay ahead. Murder, a dark and treacherous path, beckoned him with an irresistible allure. It was a fate that this particular client, in the face of their transgressions, undeniably warranted.

The arduous trek from the streets of South Wales to the bustling streets of Birmingham stretched on endlessly, as if time itself had conspired to prolong the journey. As the moon cast an ethereal glow upon the quiet suburban street, Tye skillfully manoeuvred his vehicle to a halt outside Jolene's home. With utmost care, he cradled her delicate form in his strong arms, as if she were a fragile porcelain doll. The anticipation in the air was palpable as he approached Sherry who was stood in the doorway.

The shrill ring of the telephone pierced through the stillness of the room, jolting her from her thoughts. With a sense of trepidation, she reached out and answered the call. It was one of the girls, her voice trembling with a mix of fear and urgency, delivering the grim news of Jolene's fate. Sherry, with a voice as smooth as silk, gently soothed the distressed girl on the other end. From this pivotal moment forward, she assured the girl, a vigilant doorman would stand guard at the very threshold of every house, along with another doorman inside the property.

A singular truth had remained unchallenged, no soul, in the vast expanse of their existence, had ever dared to conceive of crossing their path in such a brazen manner. However, she pondered, the notoriety of Otis remained confined within the boundaries of Birmingham. It was only a matter of time before a sinister soul would dare to test their fate against him. In the depth of her despair an insidious desire took root, a sinister longing for the demise of this client. How evil was he, to inflict harm upon a young girl.

Sherry stood frozen in the doorway, her eyes widening in horror as she beheld the sight before her. Jolene's motionless form lay in Tye's arms, her body bearing the unmistakable marks of a brutal assault. Her mind was a whirlwind of uncertainty, a tempest of conflicting thoughts. Shady and Otis, would need to be informed. Sherry was scared and she needed to pray, desperately hoping that an elusive doctor lurked within their ranks, concealed from her knowledge. In the six months she had graced their lives, she had never come across the shocking reality of their nefarious business dealings till now. Her mind was in turmoil, filled with worry. Would Jolene survive? what was she going to tell Alice? Tomorrow was her birthday; they were all meant to go on a day trip to a nearby farm. Now a shadow of apprehension loomed over the day, she hoped Alice wouldn't be too upset, if they had to cancel.

With a heavy heart and a mind burdened by the weight of impending revelations. The news, like a dagger poised to strike, would have to be delivered to Alice, in the morning, shattering her innocence once more. Sherry banished these nagging thoughts to the recesses of her mind, her focus now consumed by the task at hand. With a commanding tone, she instructed Tye to carefully place Jolene on the plush blanket adorning the sofa in the front room. Meanwhile, Sherry swiftly set about her preparations, retrieving a bowl of steaming water and a soft flannel from the airing cupboard.

In desperation, she found herself relying on Tye, to aid her in the task of cleansing Jolene's motionless form. Only then, once the harrowing task was complete, could Tye carry her to the sanctuary of her bedroom. Jolene's body was covered in burns, covered in blood, covered in bruises.

Tye sauntered into the warmth of the kitchen, his footsteps echoing off the worn linoleum floor. With a heavy sigh, he set about the task of preparing a pot of tea. His mind was burdened with the weight of the events that had unfolded. Meanwhile, Sherry knelt beside Jolene. Her hands moving with a tenderness that belied the brutality of the scene before her. Sherry's heart shattered into a million pieces, her tears falling like raindrops on a stormy night. With trembling hands, she gently cleansed Jolene's immobile form, erasing the damning evidence of the cruel torment inflicted by a sadistic client. Jolene was still unconscious and for that Sherry was grateful. Cleaning her body would cause her no untold agony. The burns, there were so many pot mark burns. Jolene was covered in them.

CHAPTER 16: The Doctor.

As the shrill ring of the telephone pierced the air, Otis's hand shot out, snatching the receiver from its cradle. Shady, his trusted accomplice, lay sprawled on a makeshift operating table in the back room, of the notorious Palmers nightclub. His face contorted in pain, as a skilled hand meticulously stitched up his wounds. Shady's keen eyes caught the subtle shift in Otis's countenance, a tell-tale sign of smouldering rage. The air around them crackled with an electric intensity as Otis's temper flared, his simmering anger threatening to boil over. After Otis replaced the receiver, he proceeded to divulge the unsettling news to Shady, skillfully manoeuvring around the grim reality that Jolene had fallen victim to the heinous crime. Otis sat at the worn wooden desk, his fingers tapping nervously against the surface.

The events of the past few days had taken a toll on their lives, leaving them entangled in a web of uncertainty and danger. With a heavy sigh, Otis picked up the vintage telephone, its cord twisted and worn from years of use. He dialled Sherry's number, the sound of each digit echoing through the room. As the phone rang, his mind raced, contemplating the words he would choose to convey the gravity of the situation. Finally, Sherry's voice crackled through the receiver, her tone filled with anticipation and concern. Otis cleared his throat, his voice steady but laced with a hint of sorrow. He began to inform her of the unfortunate news. "Sherry," he began, his voice low and sombre, " Shady's been shot. I regret to inform you that due to Shady's injuries, we won't be able to return home until late tomorrow.

The circumstances have become more complex than we could have ever imagined." A heavy silence hung in the air, the weight of their predicament pressing down on them both. Otis continued, his voice filled with a mixture of apprehension and determination.

"Furthermore, I cannot discuss with you what has happened tonight, but I know, and I promise you I will deal with it". Shady's body throbbed with an agonising ache, rendering him unable to fully grasp the words that had left Otis's lips. Shady surveyed the scene before him, his eyes narrowing with a mix of concern and curiosity. Images flashed through Otis's mind, of Jolene lying bloodied and beaten. As his mind raced to piece together the puzzle, a sudden realisation struck him like a bolt of lightning. It was not just any top girl who had suffered this heinous assault. It was Jolene, his daughter. Nobody did that, to one of his girls without his consent. The fire of revenge ravaged his thoughts once more. She was his property to do with as he wished, but for some unknown to do that to her, made him feel anger raging through his entire body. It was a revelation, normally he wouldn't care, normally he would laugh at the situation, but this was Jolene. His Jolene.

No, fate had dealt a cruel hand, for it was Jolene, the enigmatic beauty, his daughter. No one else was allowed to hurt his kin, but him. Otis concealed his smouldering rage, fully aware that his current distance from home rendered him utterly useless. The seething anger within him would be forced to bide its time. Under the cloak of darkness, Shady and Otis retreated to the confines of their hotel, seeking privacy so they could discuss this night's events. Shady's wound, wasn't life threatening, the Doctor had managed to remove the bullet and stitch him back up. With bated breath, they awaited the call from Micky Palmer, his firm were scouring the city for the shipment they had lost. In the lavish hotel room, the air thick with tension, Otis delivered the fateful news to Shady. "Jolene was hurt, seriously hurt."

Back in the family home, Sherry was fastidiously attending to Jolene, her hands delicately wiping away the remnants of the harrowing ordeal. The young girl lay motionless, her once vibrant spirit now held captive by the clutches of unconsciousness. Yet, in fleeting moments, a faint whimper escaped her lips, a haunting reminder of the torment she had endured. With due care, Sherry adorned Jolene in a flowing nightdress crafted from pure white cotton. The fabric cascaded down Jolene's figure, embracing her like a shroud of innocence.

Sherry's tear-streaked face betrayed her inner turmoil as she made her way through the hallway, her footsteps echoing against the cold hardwood floor. The scent of desperation hung heavy in the air, mingling with the faint aroma of freshly brewed coffee that wafted from the kitchen. As she entered the kitchen, the room seemed to shrink around her, the walls closing in like a vice. Tye's keen eyes caught sight of Sherry's trembling figure, her body betraying the fear that devoured her.

He swiftly closed the distance between them, his steps purposeful and determined. With a gentle but firm embrace, he enveloped her quivering form. As he held her, he enquired about the state of Jolene. "Jolene will need ample time to recover from this harrowing ordeal. It appears cigarette burns were inflicted upon her flesh; we can only hope that no lasting harm has been done. One can only surmise that the vile miscreant responsible, derived perverse pleasure from it. He must have been one sadistic bastard. She may be scarred for life. Her face remained untouched, a small mercy amid such unspeakable horror."

"Otis, has arranged for a doctor tomorrow, leaving us in suspense as to the true extent of her injuries, until he arrives." In that very moment, she succumbed to the overwhelming weight of her emotions, her tears cascading down like a torrential downpour. In the depths of despair, her voice trembled with a mixture of anguish and fury. "How could someone do this? she is barely a babe. I demand retribution, swift and merciless. I want him tortured, as he tortured my Jolene. I want the perpetrator's life extinguished, forever silenced." With a subtle gesture, Tye beckoned Sherry to settle herself upon the worn wooden chair near the kitchen table. His voice, laced with venom, resonated through the air as he uttered, "Rest assured, the bastard will pay the ultimate price". Sherry felt her heart throbbing as if a malevolent blade had mercilessly cleaved through its delicate fibres. With a subtle nod, she silently agreed. Tye was a man of his word, she trusted him.

Tonight, he would be her protector, her confidant. Her voice trembled as she blurted out, "Shady, has been shot". Otis's words echoed in her mind, haunting her with cryptic meaning. The revelation sent a chill down her spine. What had happened to Shady? And more importantly, why? The questions swirled in her thoughts; how much could one bear in a single night? It was a query that whispered through the minds of those entangled in the dark underbelly of crime and corruption. The answer, elusive yet tantalising, held the power to unravel lives, shatter illusions, and expose the raw truth. Crime didn't always pay in kind, sometimes it paid with karma. Her mind consumed by a single hope, that Shady's injuries were minor. Otis, had chosen to withhold the intricate details, leaving her to rely solely on her fervent prayers. Sherry's voice trembled as she spoke once more. "She is ready for you to take her upstairs to her bedroom, you can stay with her tonight if you like, as Otis and Shady will not be back home until late tomorrow."

Tye, consumed by worry and plagued by the weight of the impending darkness, remained perched upon a solitary chair in the dimly lit confines of Jolene's bedroom. The hours slipped away, their passage marked only by the rhythmic rise and fall of her weakened breath. With unwavering determination, he clutched her delicate hand, his touch a lifeline amidst the ebb and flow of her consciousness.

The embrace of slumber eluded him. As the first rays of dawn filtered through the intricate lace curtains, Jolene stirred from her slumber. Her body throbbed with an agonising ache, each pulse a reminder of the violence she had endured. Her lips trembled, desperately attempting to form the words that lingered on the tip of her tongue. The weight of her silence hung heavy in the air, suffocating the room with an eerie tension. Panic gripped her heart, its icy fingers tightening their hold as she came to the chilling realisation that a sinister fate had descended upon her. Tye's grip tightened around her hand, causing a surge of panic to course through her veins. The mere thought of Otis discovering their illicit connection sent shivers down her spine, casting a shadow of fear over her every move. Why was he here, he shouldn't be, it was too dangerous, he shouldn't be here.

Tye, his piercing gaze fixated on Jolene, detected her consciousness returning. With a gentle touch, he caressed her features, his robust hands providing a sense of security. In a soothing tone, he interjected, "I'm here. Please don't make any sudden movements, you were drugged and savagely beaten, just hours ago." Jolene's body lay broken and battered, aching with an intensity that made her feel as if she was being pinned down. Desperation clawed at her, urging her to rise. Yet, the pain, relentless and unyielding, held her captive, rendering her movements feeble and futile. Her voice, once strong and resolute, now faltered, and waned as she struggled to articulate her thoughts. "But Otis," she whimpered, her words dissipating into the air. Confusion clouded her mind, obscuring her understanding of the events that had led her to this harrowing realisation. A heavy sigh escaped her lips, laden with a mix of sorrow and determination. "It's Alice's birthday today," she whispered, her voice barely audible, as tears welled up in her eyes, tracing a path down her hauntingly beautiful face."

Tye's heart skipped a beat, succumbing to the profound depths of emotion that Jolene's tumultuous journey had etched upon her. Despite the relentless assault her body had endured, she remained impervious to self-concern, her sole preoccupation being the forthcoming celebration of Alice's birthday and the preservation of Tye's life. In that fateful hour, he found himself ensnared in the clutches of an irrevocable infatuation for her. He sat there, spellbound by her words, for even now, all she thought about was others. She would always put everyone else before herself. She was selfless, selfless and altruistic. Even now after everything, she had been through and suffered, she still thought about everyone else. Her beauty was a force to be reckoned with, casting a spell upon him that he couldn't resist. But it was not just her physical allure that held him in a trance, it was her selflessness, her unwavering devotion to others, that truly left him in awe. He pleaded with her to stay in bed, as he descended the stairs, intending to speak with Sherry.

Uncertain whether he should transport Jolene downstairs to the comforts of the lounge, he grappled with the decision. Sherry was preparing a hearty breakfast. The aroma of sizzling bacon and freshly brewed coffee filled the air, mingling with the anticipation of a new day. Meanwhile, in the corner of the room, Alice sat hunched over her sewing desk, her petite frame bathed in the soft glow of a single lamp. With each careful stitch, she wove together the fabric of her thoughts, her mind lost in a world of patterns and possibilities. The familiar scent of the kitchen enveloped Tye, evoking a sense of comfort and nostalgia. As he inhaled deeply, he became acutely aware of the growling emptiness in his stomach, a reminder of his neglected appetite. As he stepped into the warmth of the kitchen, a hush fell over the room, and every gaze fixated on him.

Sherry, her voice laced with concern, broke the silence with a single question, her eyes searching for answers, "How is she? will you take Jolene down to the lounge for me?". Tye's response was swift. "She's awake, but she appears to be disorientated." Worry etched across his face; Tye ascended the staircase with purpose. As he reached the door to Jolene's room, he hesitated for a moment, his hand trembling slightly before gripping the doorknob.

With a firm push, Tye entered the room, his eyes immediately drawn to the figure lying motionless on the bed. Jolene, her once vibrant spirit now subdued, lay there, her delicate frame seemingly fragile in the sunlight that filtered through the curtains. Summoning all his strength, Tye approached the bed, his heart pounding in his chest. With utmost care, he cradled Jolene in his arms, her body felt so frail. Each step was taken with caution, as Tye navigated the staircase. He carefully settled her onto the plush sofa once he reached the lounge.

Alice cautiously peered around the doorframe. Sherry's cautionary words echoed in her mind, a haunting reminder of the events that unfolded the night before. Jolene's eyes locked onto Alice, with a painful smile, Jolene beckoned her closer, "Ah, my petite mermaid, come here for your Birthday kiss.". Alice dashed across the room, in that fleeting instant, all thoughts of Jolene's pain vanished from her mind as she flung herself into Jolene's embrace. Jolene's trembling hand instinctively found her quivering lip, her teeth sinking into the tender flesh as she fought to stifle the anguished cry threatening to escape. She dared not reveal her suffering to Alice, for fear of burdening her with the weight of her own torment. Suppressing the urge to emit a startled cry, she mustered a composed facade before uttering, "Happy Birthday little sis, I'm sorry I won't be able to go with you today on the farm trip." Alice recoiled when she realised, she had hurt her sister. The words escaped her lips, laden with remorse and regret. "I didn't mean to hurt you," she confessed, her voice tinged with sorrow. The weight of her admission hung heavy in the air. "I'm sorry I forgot," she added." I won't leave you; I don't want to go visit the farm today," she declared with sincerity. In a sudden and unexpected twist, Sherry interjected, abruptly halting the conversation between the two individuals. "We have to wait for the Doctors visit anyway." In the midst of this tense atmosphere, a glimmer of hope emerged as Sherry said, "We can have your birthday party here, I've made a cake, and we have balloons." it seemed that a celebration amidst the chaos could provide a much-needed distraction. " For the time being, it would be prudent to allow Jolene to get some rest, wouldn't you agree, Alice?" Sherry arched a perfectly sculpted eyebrow as she waited for Alice to speak. "Yes, I think that would be for the best", Alice replied, honestly. Alice released Jolene from her embrace, gingerly this time. With single-mindedness, she made her way back to the sewing desk nestled in the heart of the kitchen. Jolene reclined on the plush sofa; her slender fingers were flipping idly through the myriad of channels on the remote.

Despite the vast array of entertainment at her fingertips, none of it managed to hold her attention. For deep within the recesses of her being, a searing pain gnawed at her, rendering her incapable of finding solace in the distractions of the outside world. Her body, a canvas of grotesque discolouration, bore the haunting imprints of violence. Bruises marred her once flawless skin. And there, amidst the tapestry of her suffering, were the cruel pot marks, remnants of merciless cigarette burns. They hurt, her skin hurt, her ribs hurt. Even breathing hurt. Everything hurt. Her entire being, reverberated with agony, every inch of her body crying out in torment. Against all odds, she drifted off to sleep once more. The weary hours of slumber had barely graced her restless mind when the ominous presence of the doctor materialised at her doorstep.

Sherry made her way to the front door allowing the good doctor entry to their home. With a deep breath, she turned the key and slowly swung open the door. The doctor possessed the countenance of a seasoned gentleman, his features chiselled and weathered by time. A beaky nose protruded from his face, lending an air of sharpness to his visage. His slender frame, though slightly stooped with age, exuded an undeniable elegance.

As he stepped across the threshold, Alice's heart raced in her chest. The sound of his voice sent a shiver down her spine, causing her to instinctively seek refuge behind the kitchen door. In her haste, fear gripped her so tightly that she lost control, her body betraying her with a tell-tale sign of her terror. A small puddle formed on the cold hard floor. With a heart pounding like a drum, she ascended the stairs in a frenzied sprint, her petite limbs propelling her forward with an urgency born of desperation.

Tye's eyes widened in disbelief as he stood frozen in place, his gaze fixated on the pool of urine that lay before him. The putrid stench permeated the air, assaulting his senses and causing his stomach to churn. It was a sight that defied reason. He looked at Alice, and then to the puddle of urine on the floor, then back to Alice. Why had she wet herself? The answer eluded him.

As the lounge buzzed with the hushed whispers of the doctor and Sherry attending to Jolene's fragile condition. The air was thick with the scent of antiseptic. Just as Sherry was about to delve deeper and ask about Jolene's medical predicament, a figure materialised in the doorway. Tye, approached with a sense of urgency etched upon his face. His piercing eyes bore into Sherry's, silently demanding her attention. Without a word, Tye motioned towards the kitchen, he needed to speak with her in private.

Little did Sherry know, she would be torn between her duty to Jolene and her duty to Alice. As Sherry stepped into the kitchen, her eyes immediately drawn to the ominous puddle that soaked the pristine tiles. A flicker of concern danced across her face, as she surveyed the scene before her. "What has happened here then?" she pondered aloud, her voice tinged with bewilderment. Tye's heart raced as he anxiously shifted his weight from one foot to the other. The room seemed to close in on him. "Alice cowered behind the kitchen door as the Doctor arrived. At the sound of his voice, Alice stood there and wet herself, it seemed like she was terrified". Bewildered and confused, Sherry yearned to return to the lounge, where the Doctor awaited with crucial information about Jolene's grievous wounds. In her haste, she carelessly brushed off Tye, her mind consumed by the pressing matter at hand. "I cannot attend to that presently," she uttered, her words devoid of consideration. "Once we have gleaned the Doctor's insights, I shall go see to Alice?" Tye knew something was off, with the Doctor. He couldn't put his finger on it, but his gut instinct was telling him that the Doctor had somehow terrified poor Alice. Something was wrong, very wrong.

CHAPTER 17: Creep.

As the doctor examined Jolene's wounds, Sherry couldn't shake off the unsettling sensation that crept up her spine. His eyes fixated on Jolene's nearly exposed form, a hunger evident in his gaze. Was he a creep, or was she just imagining things? With a determined effort, she suppressed the whirlwind of thoughts in her mind. Her eyes darted anxiously towards the doctor, her voice quivering with urgency as she pressed him for answers. "Tell me, doctor, will she be alright?" The doctor's gloved hand shakily lowered Jolene's Nightdress, concealing the evidence of her vulnerability. He wanted to take his time, take his time with Jolene, as the memories of a certain night shrouded his mind. The smell of her, the smell of innocence, her young skin, her body beneath him. But this woman was interrupting him, interrupting his memories, interrupting his deviant thoughts. With a voice that carried both reassurance and a hint of uncertainty, he uttered the words, "Yes, she will be okay." He hurriedly slipped a note into the warmth of her hands, a prescription for pain relief. He instructed her to make a trip to the pharmacy. Leaving behind his bottles of antiseptic liquid, on the nightstand. "You must administer it twice daily," he advised, his voice low and authoritative, "after cleansing her wounds." With a solemn air, he rose from his seat, his eyes scanning Jolene's body, one last time. He needed to leave, he needed to leave now. The fire in his groin area was rising. The weight of his decision hung heavy in the air as he politely excused himself from the confines of their home. With bated breath, she exhaled a sigh of relief on hearing the doctor close the front door behind him.

 Jolene winced, her body throbbing with pain, a result of the doctor's rough handling. Though his touch had appeared gentle, the ache that now consumed her told a different tale. Sherry's heart swelled with relief as she received the news that Jolene had emerged unscathed, her frame free from broken bones or any lingering damage. With a tender stroke of Jolene's face, she informed Jolene that she needed to see to Alice.

Tye appeared in the lounge, his presence bringing some relief to Jolene. With a sense of urgency, he inquired about the situation, his tall frame gracefully descending to the floor beside Jolene. Jolene grimaced, her eyes narrowing as she uttered the words, "There was something strangely familiar about that doctor." Tye's eyes darted nervously across the room. He pressed his teeth into his lower lip. Should he confide in Jolene, revealing the incident that unfolded in the kitchen? The answer lingered on the edge of his consciousness, tempting him with the allure of truth. A flicker of caution gleamed in his eyes, urging him to reconsider. With a heavy sigh, he chose to keep his silence, burying the truth deep within the recesses of his troubled mind. Jolene found herself burdened with a multitude of troubles, her plate overflowing with the weight of her worries. She knew that doctor, but where from? The answer eluded her. In that fateful moment, Tye's fingers closed around Jolene's delicate hand.

Jolene's countenance, etched with an indelible sense of torment, fixated upon the flickering screen of the television set. A profound darkness gnawed at her psyche, for she recognised the Doctor, the origin of this familiarity eluded her, like a shadowy figure slipping through the labyrinth in the corridors of her memory. A chilling sensation of dread coursed through her very being, causing her bones to shiver with unease. The answer, continued to elude her grasp. It was a puzzle that would only reveal itself in slumber. In fleeting moments of lucidity, she emerged from the depths of her sleep, her heart pounding with fear. A solitary tear cascaded down her exquisite countenance, a poignant testament to her anguish.

Within the recesses of her mind, the visage of the doctor transpired, his presence haunting her dreams. His malevolent sneer, dripping with depravity, seared into her consciousness. In her nightmares, a chilling revelation gripped her soul - he was one of the vile men who had paid Otis, to orchestrate unspeakable torment, inflicted upon her and her sister. In a twisted turn of events, Otis had ordered the arrival of the doctor to their home, a doctor who had raped them. How could he do this. How could, he? The malevolent nature of this act was beyond comprehension, surpassing all bounds of depravity. She was well aware of Otis's wickedness, but this latest scheme defied any semblance of reason. The realisation struck her with a force that reverberated through her very being. Her gaze fixated on the abyss, her voice piercing the void as she called out, oblivious to the fact that Tye had departed hours ago. The weight of solitude settled upon her, enveloping her in its chilling embrace. In that fateful moment, her heart raced with trepidation as she fervently beseeched the heavens, hoping against hope, that young Alice had not seen the doctor. Jolene remembered his breath, that sour breath on her skin, breathing heavily on her. It permeated the air in her dreams, only it wasn't a dream. It had happened. It was very real, the sensation of his cloying sweaty skin, against hers. The very doctor they had entrusted their lives to, had been one of the malevolent figures haunting their nightmares. In that fateful moment, a desperate yearning to be near her sister eclipsed the searing agony that gripped her frail form. Jolene's heart raced as she felt an urgent need to be by her sister's side, an unyielding desire to safeguard her from the perils that lurked in the shadows.

    The burden of responsibility pressed upon her, compelling her to act and ensure the safety of her beloved sibling. Jolene, her steps hushed and cautious, ascended the staircase, her presence barely a whisper in the dimly lit house. With aching limbs, she gingerly settled herself onto Alice's bed, as if seeking solace in its comforting embrace. It was within these four walls that she felt a semblance of security, a fragile shield against the perils that lurked in their world. The knowledge that they were united, bound by an unspoken bond, provided her with a sliver of comfort amidst the uncertainty that plagued her every waking moment.

    During these fleeting moments, their love for one another became an indisputable force. In the corners of the bedroom, Alice's voice pierced the silence, her words dripping with suspicion. "He was one of them, the doctor, wasn't he?" Jolene, her breath held in anticipation, responded in a hushed tone, her voice barely audible. "Yes, little sister, he was one of the wretched men who hurt us." With a solemn gaze, she uttered the words, her voice tinged with a mixture of determination and vulnerability. "I promise you, he will never hurt us again." The room was shrouded in an eerie silence, so thick it seemed to suffocate the very air. Two sisters, bound by an unbreakable bond, lay entwined in each other's arms, surrendering to the embrace of sleep. The dawn arrived with an abruptness that caught both the young girls off guard, its radiant rays failing to assuage the trepidation that gripped their hearts. In the depths of their own sanctuary, a shroud of fear enveloped them. Despite the comforting presence of Sherry, their protector, they knew all too well that safety remained an elusive concept, as long as Otis continued to exist within their realm. The mere notion sent shivers down their spines, a sinister dread that consumed their very essence. He, would never grant them peace, ceaselessly tormenting them until the bitter end, when either their lives were extinguished or his own.

CHAPTER 18: Home truths.

Silently, the girls descended the staircase, their footsteps barely audible against the polished wood. A collective sigh of relief escaped their lips as they entered the kitchen, to discover Sherry's graceful figure. She settled herself at the table, a glimmer of determination in her eyes. With a flick of her wrist, she beckoned them to join her. Silently vowing to unravel the questions surrounding the doctor's visit.

A chilling realisation washed over her. It was as if the weight of the world had settled upon her shoulders, burdening her with an unshakable sense of foreboding. She was acutely aware that the key to the mystery lay in the hands of these two captivating young girls, their beauty concealing a truth that sent shivers down her spine. "Girls, come here and sit with me," she uttered, her voice quivering with an undercurrent of fear. Alice stood before her, her eyes filled with a mixture of fear and uncertainty.

The events of yesterday's accident in the kitchen weighed heavily upon her conscience, and Sherry could sense her desperation to unburden herself. "Please, Alice," she implored, her voice laced with a hint of urgency, "Tell me the truth. Was it Tye who caused it all?" "NO no." Alice's words tumbled out of her mouth, her echoes fading into the air. Jolene's interruption sliced through the tense silence like a knife, shattering the fragile equilibrium that had settled over the room. Her sudden intrusion sent shockwaves rippling through the air. Sherry's eyes narrowed as she listened intently. "It was the doctor," she whispered, her voice barely audible above the pounding of her heart. Sherry's senses were abruptly assaulted, a sharp blow to her gut leaving her breathless. A sinister premonition crept through her veins, enveloping her in a shroud of unease. Undeterred, she pressed on, delving deeper into the unknown. "What do you mean?" she demanded. She posed the question, her voice laced with a hint of trepidation, as if she was tiptoeing along the edge of a precipice. Doubt gnawed at her, casting a shadow over her desire to know the truth.

Jolene's words tumbled out, a confession she knew could never be unsaid. "The doctor was one of the men who raped us. Otis, made money selling us to the highest bidders." Sherry's countenance turned ashen, a wave of nausea washing over her, as she comprehended the weight of the secret these young girls had just entrusted with her. In that very moment, Alice, her eyes brimming with tears, began to recount the events of that fateful night—the night of their mother's funeral. With a trembling voice, she delved into the depths of her memory, unveiling the intricate layers of the harrowing tale that had haunted her ever since. Jolene interjected, her voice laced with urgency. "We were drugged," she confessed, her eyes darting nervously around the room. "I didn't know that Alice had remembered it all until just now." Her words hung in the air, heavy with the weight of a long-kept secret.

Silent tears ran down her beautiful face. In a moment of profound clarity, Sherry's keen perception pierced through the veil of Jolene's tears. It was not a lamentation for her own plight that cascaded down her cheeks, but rather a poignant revelation. The weight of the truth settled upon her like a heavy fog, for Jolene had come face to face with the grim reality that her sister had endured these haunting nightmares in silence, concealing them from the world, even from her own flesh and blood. Jolene, with a determined glint in her eyes, forged ahead into the unknown. "I found myself plagued by flashbacks, vivid memories that pierced my mind. The truth had revealed itself to me with chilling clarity the morning after, when we desperately attempted to clean ourselves, wash away the shame. But our efforts were in vain, for Alice, poor Alice, didn't stop bleeding until Maria got her a doctor, not the one from yesterday." Her voice, laden with sorrow and regret, trailed off into a haunting silence.

Sherry's heart raced as she paced the kitchen, her anger growing with each passing second. The air crackled with tension, her anger simmering just beneath the surface. She knew that Otis and Shady would be arriving imminently, and her fury burned hotter than ever before.

The mere thought of allowing Otis to become entangled in a romantic relationship with her was inconceivable now, and forevermore. The truth of his heinous actions towards the innocent girls had been laid bare. The depths of her despair were unfathomable. It was imperative for her to ascertain whether Shady, her brother, possessed any knowledge pertaining to the dire predicament of the girls.

She was acutely aware that Shady possessed intimate knowledge of Jolene's clandestine exploits, a desperate attempt to placate her tyrannical stepfather. An unsettling sensation gnawed at her, suggesting that this revelation carried an air of peculiarity. A newfound comprehension washed over her, revealing the reasoning behind Jolene's unwavering resolve to engage in illicit trysts with her clientele. Jolene, with unwavering resolve, had offered herself as a sacrificial lamb, in a desperate attempt to shield Alice from the clutches of impending danger.

In that fleeting moment, Sherry's heart swelled with an indescribable affection for the girl, surpassing even the value she placed upon her own existence. Jolene's unwavering resoluteness to accompany clients had long unsettled Sherry, yet the true reason behind this behaviour remained concealed until a series of recent events unfolded. How could one so tender in years possess such profound bravery? These poor girls had been through hell, and it was all at the hands of Otis. The notion, like an anchor, burdened her thoughts, sinking them into the depths of contemplation. A revelation washed over her like a chilling wave, engulfing her senses with a newfound clarity. The enigma of Jolene's inconsolable grief, Maria, in her untimely demise, had bestowed upon Jolene a precious gift - an ally, a trusted confidante amidst the treacherous labyrinth of their lives.

Together, they had forged a bond, a sanctuary where secrets were whispered and plots against Otis were hatched. Maria possessed an uncanny understanding of Otis, that surpassed the comprehension of any other individual. Never in the wildest dreams, of Sherry's consciousness had she entertained the notion that Otis, the audacious lad of their shared youth, could metamorphose into a sinister figure, a depraved soul who trafficked his own innocent children. The very notion pierced her soul, a searing pain that cut through her like a serrated sharp knife.

CHAPTER 19: Evil.

Shady and Otis, pulled up outside and headed towards the warmth of Otis's home. Their footsteps echoed through the worn floorboards, a testament to the weariness that clung to their heavy legs. Sherry's keen eyes caught sight of Shady's arm, ensconced within a sling, and a flicker of concern danced across her face. With a voice as smooth as silk, she inquired, " Shady, what happened to your arm?" Sherry's heart skipped a beat as she absorbed the weight of his words. He uttered those chilling words, "I got shot, sis. I will be alright." Her concern surged forth like a tidal wave, propelling her to inquire, her voice trembling, "By whom?" Otis abruptly broke the intense gaze, his voice cutting through the tension. "The Palmers are relentless in their pursuit," he declared. "Rest assured, they will uncover the identities of the perpetrators in due time. They have managed to recover our pilfered stash, the guards met their untimely demise in a chaotic exchange of gunfire. So, we don't have the names of the culprits yet, but we will." Otis's keen observation skills did not fail him as he detected a subtle shift in Sherry's gaze. Those familiar eyes, once adorned with a glimmer of mischief whenever she engaged in conversation with him, now appeared devoid of their usual vitality. It gnawed at his senses, like a persistent itch in the back of his throat. Yet, he dismissed it with a flick of his hand, attributing it to nothing more than his own weary imagination.

Fatigue clung to his bones. The last few days had been relentless. The air was thick with tension as the two men locked eyes. "Only our egos got hurt, my friend?" Otis replied, his voice dripping with a mixture of defiance and intrigue. In the depths of her cunning, Sherry believed it to be far more advantageous to observe the men's reaction to Alice's unfortunate mishap. "Well," she uttered with a hint of weariness, her voice laced with a tinge of concern, "Jolene, lies confined to her bed. In her vulnerable state, Alice, insisted on staying by her side, whilst she recovers. A peculiar incident unfolded when the doctor arrived here to check on Jolene, yesterday.

On hearing the doctors voice, Alice, seemed gripped by an inexplicable fear. And in a most unfortunate turn of events, her fear manifested itself in her peeing herself, right there by the kitchen door". Sherry's gaze flitted from one man to the next, her eyes searching for the slightest flicker of emotion. With a sly grin etched upon his face, Otis revelled in his victory, only a discerning eye would detect a hint of deceit lurking behind his gaze. Shady, his countenance fraught with apprehension, only displayed an air of deep concern.

The tell-tale signs etched upon their faces revealed a tale of deceit and treachery, leaving no room for doubt in Sherry's mind. She knew that confronting Shady would have to wait until the menacing presence of Otis was no longer a threat. As her heart plummeted, descending into the abyss of the ocean's depths, a surge of loathing consumed her, directed solely towards Otis.

Every fibre of her being pulsated with an intense and vehement detestation. She pondered, her mind consumed by a singular purpose: to exact a fitting retribution upon this man, a retribution that would leave an indelible mark upon his wretched soul. The heinous acts he had committed against those innocent girls would not go unpunished, for she was determined to ensure that justice prevailed. Sherry, though lacking Maria's resourcefulness, possessed a remarkable intellect. In that moment, she realised that a methodical scheme must be devised to expunge this man from their lives.

Six long weeks had passed since Jolene's body had been ravaged by the merciless hands of her assailant. The wounds had finally closed, leaving behind a haunting reminder of the brutality she had endured - pot marks that marred her once flawless, creamy complexion. Jolene and Sherry exchanged secretive whispers, formulating plans. However, as they deliberated, no concrete plans had materialised thus far. The path to vengeance remained elusive. Sherry did not know the extent of Otis's intricate web of connections.

Jolene possessed an uncanny familiarity with the labyrinth of Otis's influence, a knowledge that delved deep into the recesses of his criminal empire. She was privy to the inner workings of his adversaries, the alliances he forged with his associates, and even the identities of those who dared to betray others, acting as his eyes and ears within the treacherous underbelly of the city. Jolene and Maria had laid the groundwork long before Sherry entered their lives. In the city, where corruption thrived like a poisonous vine, it appeared that even the guardians of the law had succumbed to Otis's payroll. A network of deceit and betrayal, carefully woven by the cunning crime lord, ensnared all those who dared to oppose him.

There remained one solitary figure, a lone sentinel of justice, untainted by the stain of Otis's influence. He was a detective, renowned for his steadfast determination to bring down the nefarious activities of Otis. Time and time again, he had embarked on a perilous endeavour, each one, a valiant attempt to dismantle the intricate web of crime woven, by his elusive nemesis.

The detective's animosity towards Otis ran deep, whispered rumours circulating through the city's underbelly suggested a torrid affair between the lawman and a destitute woman of the streets, whose life was tragically cut short. The detective harboured an unspoken suspicion that Otis was connected to the untimely demise of his beloved. The notion of a lawman entangled in a forbidden liaison with a denizen of the streets struck them as peculiar, to say the least. The detective had been abruptly transferred to an undisclosed location under the orders of his commanding officer. Jolene and Tye, with an insatiable thirst for answers, were tireless in their efforts and were solely focused on trying to find the detective's whereabouts.

Regrettably, Detective Frost had proven to be quite elusive. Jolene, with a heavy heart, continued to guard her knowledge regarding Otis's peculiar assortment of hair. She clung to her mother's precious lock, determined to preserve it solely for herself, as it stood as the sole remnant of her beloved mother's existence. As her thoughts surged like a torrent of ocean waves, she couldn't contain herself as she posed the question to Sherry, her voice trembling with curiosity, " Sherry, what does the phrase 'dead yarn' mean?"

Sherry's mind swirled with confusion, her eyes darting nervously as she grappled with the question. Despite her inner turmoil, she summoned the courage to respond with honesty. "It means," she began, her voice tinged with a hint of trepidation, "a life extinguished, a soul departed from this mortal coil." Sherry's perfectly arched eyebrow ascended, a silent signal that sent a shiver down Jolene's spine.

Momentarily, a chilling transformation overcame Jolene, as if the very essence of life had been sucked out of her. The colour drained from her face, leaving behind a ghostly pallor that betrayed her inner demons. " Where did you hear such a thing, my child?" Sherry inquired, her countenance betraying a perplexed state. Jolene, her eyes darting with a hint of nervousness, refused to relinquish her secret. With a quickness that betrayed her cunning, she retorted, her voice laced with ambiguity, "Oh, it's merely something I've overheard Otis say." Jolene retreated hastily to the confines of her room, her heart pounding in her chest. She was determined not to betray the suspicions brewing within her.

The weight of the revelation bore down upon her, causing her mind to race. Could it be possible? A chilling thought gripped her soul - every lock of hair she had discovered, meticulously preserved, now took on a sinister significance. Were they the remnants of deceased women, victims of Otis's murderous fury?

Jolene forcefully suppressed the chilling realisation that had gripped her, refusing to succumb to its sinister allure. "Don't be foolish," she admonished herself, mustering every ounce of her willpower to regain composure. Having endured the brutal assault inflicted on her by that evil client, she found herself grappling with an overwhelming sense of paranoia, akin to a relentless spectre haunting her every step.

The fateful night had left an indelible mark upon her, a haunting transformation that rendered her ill-prepared, to confront the harsh realities of the outside world once more. Yet, deep within the recesses of her consciousness, a nagging sense of justice gnawed at her very core.

Time was slipping through her fingers like sand, and she could ill afford to delay any longer. Otis, with his commanding presence, would inevitably exert his influence, compelling her to return to work the parties, in due time. A sinister notion coursed through her veins, sending icy tendrils of spine-tingling terror down her back. She stood there, her heart pounding in her chest, her eyes darting nervously around the room. She was having another panic attack. The folder. Otis. Her wounds. Her sister, she needed to breathe, she needed to breathe. She knew deep down that she wasn't prepared for what lay ahead, but the question lingered in her mind, would she ever be truly ready?

CHAPTER 20: Broken wings.

If she failed to return, what would be the consequences? In her mind's eye, Otis stood before her, his eyes burning with a sinister intensity. Would he dare to unleash his wrath on her, or would he opt for a more cunning approach? The thought of being replaced by Alice, her heart sank at the mere notion. No, he wouldn't do that, surely, she thought, desperately clinging to a glimmer of hope.

The mere thought terrified her, urging Jolene to pull herself together. The words echoed through her mind. "Your sister needs you." Her determination to shield Alice from harm's way, was urging her to imprison her thoughts within the recesses of her mind, sealing it away like classified documents in a steel filing cabinet. The key, once discarded, would ensure that the secrets remained forever concealed. She couldn't give up now, she had to stay strong, strong for Alice.

With every fibre of her being, she knew she must summon the strength to press forward. In Jolene's troubled mind, a sinister notion took hold. It whispered to her. "Lock it away Jolene". With a heavy heart, she resolved to lock these dark secrets away, within the recesses of their conscience, and cast the key into the abyss of oblivion. Jolene's mind swirled with a whirlwind of thoughts, each one a delicate secret she held close to her chest. Just then, like a glimmer of light emerging from the darkness, Alice made her entrance.

Alice had faithfully stood by her side throughout the arduous journey of recovery. She had indeed assumed the role of a devoted caretaker, yearning for her sister's convalescence. Every night, without fail, they would come together, their bodies entwined, seeking refuge from the harsh realities that plagued their waking hours. In the safety of their shared bed, they found comfort in each other's arms. Alice's gaze fixated on her sister's countenance, her eyes filled with a mixture of concern and determination. With a soft, yet resolute tone, she uttered, "I am well aware that you save me from the bad men. If it were within my power, I would willingly exchange our roles in an instant."

Like a phoenix, Jolene emerged, rising from the ashes of her dark thoughts, her senses heightened. With a trembling hand, she reached out and shook Alice, her voice quivering yet resolute. "Alice," she implored, her words laced with an unyielding frustration, "never must I hear you utter those words again. Promise me, I beg you." As her tear-streaked countenance bore witness to her silent anguish, the gravity of the situation hit them both. Jolene's voice resonated with an unmistakable sense of desperation.

Alice's eyes glistened with a sorrowful glimmer, her heart heavy with remorse. The unintended consequence of her words had wounded her sister's fragile emotions. In truth, Alice harboured no ill intentions; her desire to exchange their positions was merely an expression of her profound empathy. With a solemn gaze, she looked deep into Jolene's eyes and uttered these words, her voice full of remorse. "I promise, I'm sorry," The room fell silent, the weight of Alice's voice was but a whisper, lost amidst her own sobs. With a desperate fervour, she flung her arms around her sister, their tiny frames consumed by the overwhelming grip of desperation. In a timeless embrace, forging a connection that transcended words. It was as if the universe itself held its breath, witnessing the unspoken bond that formed between them. In that fleeting instant, their souls intertwined, with understanding and empathy.

Jolene's heart raced like a runaway train as she stepped into the awaiting car, her nerves threatening to consume her. It had been months since she had last ventured out the family home. But amidst the chaos of her anxious thoughts, one glimmer of hope emerged, Tye, her trusted ally, would be her driver through this night. Amidst the tumultuous trials that had befallen her, Tye had managed to reclaim his role as her trusted chauffeur.

Jolene, if she dared to confront her own vulnerability, found herself consumed by an unfamiliar sensation - fear. Once a fearless soul, she now harboured a lingering anxiousness that threatened to shatter her resolve. Determined to safeguard her well-being, she vowed to adopt a newfound caution, clutching tightly to her own personal bottle. She would decline any drinks offered at the house parties, ensuring she would never be drugged again.

Jolene could not bear the burden of the other girl's well-being as well, they would still have to take drinks from the strange men that frequented the parties. Her own psyche remained in a precarious and delicate condition. Otis had unleashed his menacing words on her, whilst ensuring that Sherry had remained oblivious to their sinister conversations. With a calculated manipulation, he coerced her, compelling her to return to the treacherous world she had briefly escaped. With a chilling air of authority, he issued a menacing ultimatum: comply with his every command or face the dire consequences.

The stakes were high, for failure to comply would result in Alice, an innocent soul, being thrust into a world of debauchery against her will. Jolene's senses tingled with an ominous foreboding, a subtle shift in Sherry's demeanour towards Otis had been evident. A chill ran down her spine, for she knew the danger, if she could perceive this change, then surely Otis, with his cunning instincts, had also taken notice.

The bond that once united them, had been severed. Jolene's mind was consumed by the folder, its contents haunting her thoughts. The collection of hair within its confines held a power over her, one that demanded her attention. She yearned to confide in someone, to seek their counsel on the matter. The weight of those foreboding words, "dead yarn," in the dark recesses of her mind, every waking moment.

Sherry had revealed its significance to Jolene. From that moment onward, an unsettling sensation clung to her, refusing to release its grip. In the depths of her consciousness, a chilling realisation took hold: Otis, was the perpetrator behind those heinous crimes that had plagued the city. Yet, burdened by the weight of this damning knowledge, she found herself entangled in a web of uncertainty. Who could she trust?

Jolene's eyes darted away to the passing streets, her attention momentarily stolen by the distant sound of a siren wailing through the night. She turned her gaze back to the man before her, his voice laced with urgency as he repeated his question. "Jolene, are you listening to me?" Tye's voice pierced through the thick veil of Jolene's brooding, jolting her back to reality.

Her mind was abruptly shaken by his words. Tye, a keen observer, couldn't help but notice the aura that surrounded Jolene in recent days. Her distant gaze and detached demeanour spoke volumes, hinting at her journey through the depths of despair. Tye's heart sank as he sensed the girl he had once cherished slipping away from his grasp.

The tendrils of love that had entwined their souls, now seemed to unravel, leaving him with a hollow ache in his chest. Tye couldn't help but wonder if he was witnessing the tragic demise of a love story, that had once burned with an intensity unmatched. With resolve, he vowed to resurrect her spirit, to reignite the flickering flame that had captivated him from the moment they crossed paths." I shall wait here all night for you, till you've finished. I have also enlisted my friend Anton to be your personal guard, he's in the house already. Please be careful Jolene." Jolene's response came at last, her voice laced with a hint of frustration. "But Otis," she uttered, her words dripping with exasperation, "he refuses to allocate any more funds for additional guards." Tye's interruption sliced through the air, with a hint of defiance. "I must stop you there," he declared, his eyes locked on hers. "Shady and I, we footed the bill." As the sleek black sedan glided to a halt outside the imposing Victorian house in the heart of Worcester, Tye's grip tightened around Jolene's delicate hand. His voice, laced with a mixture of concern and anticipation, pierced the tense silence that enveloped them. "I love you," he whispered, his words barely audible above the rhythmic hum of the engine. "My stomach churns with unease, but I know you can do this." Jolene's piercing gaze locked onto Tye's, her eyes revealing a depth of emotion that he desperately sought to penetrate. He could sense her inner turmoil, her guarded heart resisting his feeble attempts to assuage her pain. Yet, despite his earnest intentions, his efforts proved futile, unable to breach the impenetrable fortress of her sorrow. She felt broken, but a fleeting desire emerged within her, a desperate longing to escape the clutches of their grim reality. Jolene's heart pounded in her chest as she contemplated the dire predicament that lay before her.

Otis would be relentless in his pursuit if she were to run. Abandoning Alice, her sister, was simply inconceivable. "Stop it Jolene, just stop it," another voice whispered in her head. Jolene's delicate hands trembled as she presented the bottle, a silent plea for understanding. Her voice, meek and fragile, barely carried her words. "I assure you, I won't allow such a thing to happen to me again." With a swift and graceful movement, she spun on her heels, her lustrous locks dancing in the wind. Like a phantom, she vanished into the door of the party house, leaving behind a devastated Tye in her wake.

CHAPTER 21: The detective

Time had slipped away, like sand through an hourglass, with it brought the healing of Jolene's tormented soul. The haunting memories of that fateful night had etched themselves upon her fragile psyche, leaving indelible marks of anguish. Sherry had stumbled on a potion capable of erasing the remnants of Jolene's harrowing ordeal - the cruel imprints left by the scorching embers of the cigarettes. As her emotions ebbed and flowed, the scars on her skin appeared to fade along with her poor mental health.

Tye had become her guiding light in the aftermath of that fateful night. Together, they had navigated her grief, slowly piecing together the fragments of her mind and soul. As the sun began to peek through the storm clouds of her sorrow, she found herself sharing laughter once more with Tye, a testament to the resilience of the human spirit. They ventured out to dine at quaint cafes, their rendezvous shrouded in secrecy. As Otis tirelessly shuttled between Nottingham and their hometown, a web of deception spun around him, concealing the undeniable intimacy that blossomed between Tye and Jolene. Tye remained steadfast in his promise. He would always love her. He would wait for her, he would save her from this life.

The sheer force of his will was tested, to its limits as he resisted the overwhelming temptation, to press his lips against hers in that very moment when her laughter filled the air. Jolene, on the cusp of her fourteenth birthday, lingered in his thoughts. He reminded himself, with a mix of anticipation and restraint, that a mere two years stood between them, and their freedom.

He exhaled a sigh of relief, his heart swelling, she had managed to conquer her demons. Doubt had plagued his mind, with the uncertainty of her resilience, but she had succumbed to his charm once again. A nagging unease gnawed at him, for she had entrusted him with a secret of utmost importance - the folder. The object concealed locks of hair within, each strand whispering secrets of its own. Did its contents, hold the key to their salvation?

Tye anxiously sought his father's counsel. With a furrowed brow, he implored, "Dad, what should I do with this knowledge?" His father, a man of few words, met his gaze with a steely glare. "Stay well clear son," he uttered, his voice laced with a hint of caution. The emotive words of his father lingered in his mind. A dreadful premonition gnawed at his conscience, suggesting that Otis, had perpetrated a far greater number of heinous acts against innocent women than anyone was aware of. He yearned to lay his eyes upon the coveted folder, but he still couldn't risk entering Otis's house.

Jolene's heart sank as regret washed over her like a relentless tide. Oh, how she wished to turn back time and erase the moment she had foolishly confided in Tye about the ominous folder. The weight of her mistake settled upon her shoulders, a burden she could no longer bear. He pleaded with her, his eyes filled with desperation, urging her to give it him. But Jolene, trembling with fear, remained paralysed, unable to summon the courage to comply. She was acutely aware that the absence of it, once discovered by Otis upon his return, would undoubtedly seal her fate with an irrevocable, death sentence.

Unbeknownst to her, Tye had concealed his intentions to deliver the coveted folder to the esteemed detective Frost, whom he had tirelessly pursued. He had found him working in the gritty streets of Nottingham, then they had maintained a connection, their voices intertwining through the crackling static of late-night phone calls. The weight of his secret alliance with the detective hung heavily upon him, threatening to snuff out his very existence. The fear of losing Jolene, his beloved, eclipsed any concern he harboured for his own well-being. Detective Frost, with a heavy heart burdened by secrets, had entrusted Tye with a revelation that pierced through the night like a dagger.

The lifeless body of the young woman, brutally extinguished on the unforgiving streets, was not the detective's lover, but rather his own flesh and blood - a sister gone astray. His conviction was firm, a resolute belief that Otis's sinister intent, was the one responsible for her untimely demise. The evidence, though circumstantial, pointed to him like an accusing finger, leaving no room for doubt in his mind. Otis had been seen lurking around her apartment, and on the street that she worked. His dear sister had been missing her tongue, just like many other working girls whose bodies had been discarded like trash on the streets.

Detective Frosts sister had firmly rebuffed Otis's advances. Undeterred by her rejection, Otis's sinister ambitions took hold, his mind consumed by a nefarious desire to transform her into a pawn in his sordid game of exploitation. Two nights prior to her untimely demise, she had entrusted her deepest secrets to none other than her own flesh and blood, her brother. With trembling lips and a haunted look in her eyes, she confessed her deepest fear - the terror that plagued her every waking moment.

The mere thought of Otis, attacking her every nerve. What unspeakable horrors awaited her at his hands? Detective Frost, with an air of intrigue, discreetly divulged to Tye a crucial piece of information that had the power to shatter the very foundations of law and order.

Among those entangled in this web of corruption was none other than Detective Frost's former superior, a man who had once commanded respect and authority within the ranks. In the depths of his intuition, he harboured a chilling suspicion that his ex-superior possessed an unsettling predilection for the innocence of young girls. Each time he chanced upon his boss in the proximity of young girls, a startling transformation would seize him, his countenance contorting and a peculiar haze descending upon his eyes.

Detective Frost, a relentless pursuer of justice, found himself perilously close to unravelling the intricate web of human trafficking. However, as fate would have it, his determination had incurred the wrath of those in power. In a calculated move to silence his probing inquiries, Frost was abruptly stripped of his rank and relocated, far removed from the heart of the investigation.

Frost, with his keen eye for detail, maintained a vigilant surveillance on the Palmer firm. His pulse quickened, betraying his inner thrill, upon discovering the tantalising connection between Otis and this notorious firm. In the depths of his thoughts, he pondered upon the fortuitous turn of events, fervently hoping that his recent employer possessed a moral compass far less askew than his previous superior. He had unearthed hidden caches, discovered the secret haunts of debauchery, and diligently followed Palmers' illicit activities, spanning across the exotic landscapes of Trinidad and Jamaica. Frost's superior, a woman of undeniable authority, exuded an air of determination, an unmistakable aura of integrity that surrounded her. Within the depths of her soul, a profound loathing for the Palmers festered, concealed from prying eyes. The origins of this animosity remained a mystery, known only to her. Relentlessly, she persisted in goading Frost to intensify his surveillance efforts on the unsuspecting gang. He had toiled ceaselessly. Gratitude washed over Frost as his newly appointed superior had not burdened him with the weight of a partner. A creeping intuition slithered through his mind, whispering of a profound mistrust harboured by his new boss, towards those under her command. Did she harbour a suspicion that a handful of her officers had been bought off.

Tye had driven up to Nottingham several times to meet Frost. At a mere twenty years old, he possessed a wisdom that belied his youth. The young lad extended his hand, a desperate plea for assistance in dismantling the formidable Otis. Tye, with a heavy heart, finally mustered the courage to confide in Frost, revealing his predicament involving Jolene. As Frost gazed upon Tye, his eyes filled with admiration for the care, the man displayed towards Jolene. Though a sense of unease crept into his bones, for deep within his gut, he knew that Otis, a man of formidable character, had skillfully eluded the clutches of the law and his adversaries for countless years, leaving behind a trail of unanswered questions and unsolved deaths in his wake. Frost couldn't deny the gnawing worry that consumed him, his mind plagued with thoughts for the boy's safety.

He was acutely aware that they were all pawns in a treacherous game, one where the stakes were impossibly high. However, he pondered, contemplating the notion that the lad's hands were far from clean. After all, he had been complicit in chauffeuring innocent young girls for Otis. Thus, he reasoned, it would hardly be a significant tragedy if the lad were to become an unfortunate casualty in the grand scheme of things. Even though the boy had become an invaluable asset to him, a conduit of information regarding Otis and the elusive Palmers.

CHAPTER 22: Vengeance is mine.

As the moon cast an ethereal glow upon the city, Frost prepared himself for a night of relentless surveillance, his senses sharpened, and his instincts honed. But just as he was about to leave for his mission, a shrill, piercing ring shattered the tranquilly of his home, jolting him from his focused state. As his clunky strong fingers grasped the receiver, a faint crackle resonates through the line. "It's, Tye," the voice on the other end whispers. "I have information, pertaining to the death of your sister." His voice reverberated through the stillness. His voice quivered with uncertainty as he uttered the words, "Only there's a folder, I haven't seen it." the weight of his confession baring down on him. His eyes darted nervously, betraying the fear that gripped his soul. Frost leaned forward, his piercing gaze fixed upon the receiver in his hand. "Jolene, spoke of a diary, a folder, it's like a diary, with locks of hair, each one stored and stapled in little plastic sealed bags.' His voice trembled.

Frost's senses heightened, a chill coursing through his veins, as if an ominous presence had brushed against his very soul. Impatience dripped from his voice as he demanded, "Can you retrieve it?"

"Might take me some time," Tye murmured, his voice low and filled with anticipation. "But I think so, yes." The room fell silent, once more. "Don't keep me waiting too long, will you?". As the final words escaped his lips, Frost gently replaced the receiver. A sense of liberation washed over him, lifting the heavy veil that had shadowed his soul for far too long. Exiting his home, he ventured into the night, a newfound buoyancy guiding his every step. It was a sensation he hadn't experienced in years, a glimmer of hope amidst the darkness that had consumed his existence.

Sherry, plagued by an unshakable sense of unease, had become adept at evading the presence of Otis. The mere thought of his company sent shivers down her spine, compelling her to distance herself from him at all costs. He had made countless attempts in the past few months to engage in a flirtatious dance with her, yet she remained resolute in her refusal to succumb to his advances. Her eyes were opened to the sinister depths of his depravity. It was a chilling realisation. She understood, with a newfound clarity, that her paramount duty was to shield the innocent girls from his wicked ways. Yet, his very presence instilled fear in her, igniting an instinctual repulsion within her. Dinners and bookkeeping times, seemingly mundane activities, had become her pet hate. She found herself, forced to maintain a facade of affection towards him.

Amidst the dimly lit ambiance of the kitchen, she skilfully concealed her true feelings. But, every month, like clockwork, they would go through the bookkeeping together. In this intimate setting, devoid of prying eyes, Otis would make several advances towards her. He, a cunning and manipulative character, possessed an insatiable desire to make physical contact with her, using any excuse that presented itself. She, a woman of strength and resilience, questioned how much longer she could maintain her facade, of courage in the face of his advances. The fact that the young girls relied on her to maintain Otis's conduct, did nothing to appease the repugnance that was gradually eroding her strength.

Once again, Shady and Otis found themselves back in the streets of Nottingham. The Palmer Firm had summoned them, their presence required at the exclusive confines of their club. Tension hung heavy in the air as one of the Palmers clutched the envelope containing the vital intel. It was a matter of life and death, and time was running out. The fate of their futures rested on the information concealed within those folded pages. It had been passed to them from a Chief Superintendent. Shady, had unwittingly descended further into the realm of narcotics and femme fatales. The devastating impact of Maria's demise had left him bereft. The weight of her demise bore down upon him with an intensity he had never fathomed, fragmenting his spirit. Overcome by an insatiable desire to numb his anguish, he sought relief in his vices, using illicit substances to obliterate any trace of her presence.

In his reckless pursuit of temporary oblivion, he sought carnal encounters devoid of emotional connection, seeking the warmth of anyone who could offer a fleeting distraction from the pain that plagued his soul. He remained unable to confess to his own heart, the truth that he had harboured affection for her. Through the passage of time, their bond had grown impenetrable, forged by shared experiences and an unspoken kinship. Their connection ran deep, like the roots of an ancient tree, anchoring them to one another with an indomitable strength.

A profound understanding existed between them, a silent language that transcended mere words. He had never succumbed to her allure, never allowed his lips to meet hers in a passionate embrace. She was a woman ensnared in the treacherous grip of addiction, a functioning heroin addict, as they called it. There existed a breed of individuals who possessed an uncanny ability to navigate the treacherous terrain of addiction. Maria, a woman of many talents, was one such soul, who had mastered the delicate art of handling her chosen poison. Shady pondered the possibility that her refusal to administer the substance through injection, opting instead to inhale it with a pipe, might have been the reason.

As their car glided to a halt in front of the infamous Palmers club, a deathly silence enveloped the air, the normally vibrant street was doused in unsettling stillness. Not a single note of music resonated through the night, nor were there any signs of the usual throng of eager patrons eagerly anticipating a night of revelry. Otis fixed his eyes on Shady, with a steely gaze. In unison, the two men inspected their firearms, ensuring their weapons were primed for the impending encounter. With a shared understanding, they emerged from the vehicle, ready to face whatever awaited them. "Before we go in Shady, I have to warn you, someone is stealing from the Palmers, and they think it's us ". Shady's face contorted into a grimace, his eyes narrowing with suspicion. "So, they think we know something," he muttered through gritted teeth. Shady had transformed into many things in recent times, but a thief was not among them. With a menacing snarl, Otis uttered, "Let us bring this sordid affair to its bitter end, shall we?" With calculated steps, the two men infiltrated the club, slipping through the unassuming side entrance.

A henchman under Palmer's command stood guard, his presence a testament to the gravity of the situation. With an air of authority, he demanded that they submit to a thorough pat-down, his eyes scanning their every move. Reluctantly, they complied, their expressions betraying a mix of annoyance and disdain. Otis could hardly conceal his disgust at the audacity of this intrusion. As they gripped their guns they were filled with suspicion and apprehension. For quite some time now, they had been frequenting this place, armed to the teeth. The burly man, his imposing figure casting a shadow over the room, regarded Otis with a knowing look, his eyes betraying a hint of sympathy. With a voice as gruff as gravel, he uttered those chilling words, "I'm merely following orders." With a commanding tone, he beckoned Otis and Shady to follow him. The trio stealthily made their way towards the secluded offices nestled at the rear of the imposing building.

Shady's senses prickled with an uneasiness. The absence of their weapons irritated his very core, leaving him vulnerable and exposed. A chilling awareness settled upon him, as if a target had been painted upon his back, inviting danger to descend upon him like a predator stalking its prey. With an air of nonchalance, Otis sauntered through the dimly lit club, his eyes scanning the room for any signs of trouble. He followed the doorman, his footsteps barely making a sound on the polished floor.

As Otis and Shady cautiously stepped into the dark confines of the Palmer firm's main office, they noted a scene out of a horror movie. Shady's gaze fixated on two figures, their bodies slumped in the chairs positioned before the imposing desk. Bound by ropes that dug into their flesh, these unfortunate souls bore the unmistakable signs of torture. - blood seeping from their wounds, staining the floor with crimson tales of pain and suffering.

A worn wooden table stood as the sole witness to their plight. A tool bag, weathered and stained, lay abandoned upon its surface. In a moment of revelation, Shady's mind was struck with the realisation that the tool bag in question belonged to none other than Otis himself. Puzzled, he pondered the perplexing question of why Otis would willingly allow the Palmers to make use of it. However, as the seconds ticked by, the truth began to seep into Shady's consciousness, like a slow-dawning realisation. And then, like a bolt of lightning, he recognised one of the men bleeding out before him, A suffocating grip of terror constricts his very being, as the realisation dawns upon him - it was Tye. Shady's heart sank as an ominous premonition washed over him.

He knew all too well that he would be forced to bear witness to Otis's sadistic acts, of torment upon these unfortunate souls. The weight of the impending horror settled upon his shoulders. He would soon be left with the unenviable duty of recounting the ghastly events that unfolded within these walls to Jolene and Tye's father. His mind raced, consumed by a desperate craving for relief. "God, I need a drink," he mused silently.

Tension filling the room as the words escaped his lips. "What the bloody hell, is going on here?" his voice laced with a mixture of disbelief and frustration. The question echoed through the room, bouncing off the mahogany wood and the velvet wallpaper. Behind the imposing desk, a Palmer sibling loomed, brandishing a pair of pliers stained with its victim's blood.

With a sinister smile, he taunted, "It appears that these foolish imbeciles believed they could outsmart us. I believe the lad is under your employment." Shady's head bobbed in a subtle gesture, a calculated move to avoid locking eyes with Tye. With a cautious step, the Palmer boss, closed the distance between himself and the desk, the words spilled from his lips, heavy with suspicion. "Ah, but the other, my dear Otis, is a friend of yours I believe," He played with his words which were dripping in sarcasm. Otis beamed a wide smile barring his perfect white teeth, "No friend of mine, my nemesis maybe," his voice trailing off. "Well, we thought we would do you a favour, as these two were conspiring against you, the copper has been tailing us for quite some time, and the lad has been giving him intel".

Otis, consumed by a surge of rage, found himself unable to restrain his volatile emotions any longer. With a calculated and deliberate motion, he gravitated towards the tool bag, extracting a serrated-edged implement. Without hesitation, he plunged it into the unsuspecting officer's abdomen, relishing in the visceral sensation of the man's life force ebbing away. The tide of blood drenching Otis's hands and saturating the floor.

Otis had harboured a deep-seated desire for the demise of this man, Detective Frost, for an interminable stretch of time. And in a mere blink of an eye, that desire was fulfilled, leaving the detective extinguished from existence. As Otis prepared to make his move on Tye, his target. The atmosphere crackled with anticipation, the silence broken only by the faint sound of their breaths. But just as

Otis was about to pounce, a commanding figure emerged from the shadows, halting him in his tracks. It was none other than another member of the Palmer hierarchy, a man known for his ruthlessness and cunning.

His mere presence sent a shiver down Shady's spine, as he realised the gravity of the situation. The room fell into an eerie stillness, as the two men locked eyes, a silent battle of wills unfolding before them. Otis, with a calm and deliberate demeanour, took a moment to collect himself. "Take your time Otis," his voice laced with venom. "I think you'll find he has valuable information." Otis's lips curled into a sinister sneer. "What could this boy possess," his voice dripping with malice, "that I so desperately require?" The Palmer Boss extended a towel to Otis, urging him to clean his hands of the evident blood stains. With a calculated motion, one of the Palmers then presented Otis with an envelope. Silently, Otis took hold of the envelope, his fingers still covered in the detective's blood.

As Otis tore open the envelope, the room seemed to hold its breath, as if anticipating the revelation that lay within. With the following words etched on the paper.

'Detective Aiden Frost and Tye Jamal have been plotting against you and your business associate, Otis Charles, for some time now. Since the detective has generously documented your every move, you should immediately alter your routes, stash locations, and shipment details. In his notes, there was also information about a folder belonging to Otis that may contain evidence of the death of the detective's sister. The folder could result in arrests. I propose burning the folder to eliminate any incriminating evidence. This could have brought down the entire house of cards if I hadn't intervened. Always acting in your best interests, D.C.'

CHAPTER 23: Deadly encounters.

Tye's entire being quivered with an instinctual recoil, each blow landing with merciless precision, assaulting his body with unrelenting force. In the throes of his final moments, a kaleidoscope of memories surged through his mind. In the chaos, his thoughts lingered on the figure of his father, a pillar of strength and guidance. Though it was Jolene, the girl who had captured his heart, that held an even more profound place in his thoughts. He should have kissed her. He should have done more to save her, but fate had other plans. Their paths, so tantalisingly close, never converged in the intimacy of love. His heart ached with the missed opportunity, aching for the touch that would forever evade him. As his life blood ebbed away, his final cognitions were consumed by a single thought, to safeguard his Jolene. Otis seethed with frustration as his anticipation of inflicting torment upon the lad was abruptly thwarted.

Tye's final breath escaped his lips, leaving behind a charred and disfigured body, a testament to the ruthless combination of alcohol-induced waterboarding and the merciless act of setting him ablaze. Otis had cultivated a predilection for this particular modus operandi, honed through his encounters with the brothers he had eliminated in the sun-soaked streets of Trinidad. It had become a ritual. With a callousness that chilled the soul, he doused his hapless victim in whatever volatile spirit he could lay his hands on, and then he would watch them scream in agonising torture.

As the flickering flames leapt and twirled, a grotesque ballet of destruction, he stood there, an unholy spectator, relishing the sight of their flesh igniting and liquefying. And just when the torment seemed unbearable, he would abruptly extinguish the inferno with a bucket of water, leaving his prey gasping for breath, their charred skin clinging to their bones. Patiently, he would bide his time, waiting for the desiccated remnants to dry, only to repeat his sadistic actions with a perverse satisfaction that defied reason. Tye's refusal to implicate others, ignited a rage within Otis. Shady observed the young boy's harrowing plight, his heart pounding with trepidation. Every fibre of Shady's being, was praying for the lad to guard his secrets, to keep them hidden from Otis. For if the boy were to divulge the truth, it would spell doom for every one of them, a certain death sentence.

The acrid scent of seared flesh permeated the office, assaulting Shady's olfactory receptors. In the depths of Shady's conscience, a glimmer of relief flickered as the boy's life was extinguished, perhaps more swiftly than the rest of the room had hoped. Deep down, Shady was in a quandary, he didn't want the boy to be murdered. But his blood boiled as he discovered that the young lad had turned out to be a treacherous informant, feeding valuable intel to the authorities.

"I must confess, Shady," Otis's voice was dripping with a calculated edge, "the Palmers are well aware that we, as seasoned criminals, would never stoop so low as to pilfer from them. After all, there exists an unspoken code of honour among our kind." The words escaped his lips, dripping with silent innuendo's. A subtle smirk played at the corners of his mouth, betraying a hint of amusement. "I was testing you" he drawled, with a sinister charm. "A test to ascertain your loyalty, for it was you who had enlisted the lad into our fold. However, I must extend my sincerest apologies." Otis arched an eyebrow, as his gaze fixed on Shady. "You're like a brother to me," Shady pleaded, his voice filled with desperation. "What kind of daft scenario is that? "Shady, with a quick and calculated move, skillfully deflected the insinuations that Otis had thrown his way. Shady's eyes, sharp and piercing, betrayed no hint of vulnerability as he skillfully evaded Otis's attempts. His heart pounding within his chest, a traitorous accomplice threatening to expose him, with each thunderous beat.

Jolene's heart pounded with unease as the hours stretched into days, her worry growing like a dark cloud on the horizon. Tye, had vanished without a trace, leaving her with a gnawing sense of dread. The absence of his presence weighed heavily on her mind. What had become of Tye? The uncertainty was eating away at her, fuelling her determination to uncover the truth behind Tye's mysterious absence.

When she had asked him what was wrong, he just assured her, "nothing to trouble your pretty little head with."

Those words did nothing to alleviate her fears. An ominous sensation ripping through her core. Tomorrow she would speak with Sherry, asking her if she could ascertain his whereabouts. Tye had only ever been away for two days before, to visit family. Jolene wished this night would be over swiftly. Her sole objective was to ensure the seamless execution of the party, leaving no room for mishaps. Once she had finished, she could leave the party earlier than usual, so she could get some much-needed sleep. It was her fourteenth birthday tomorrow and she, Sherry and Alice were all going to the local farm on a daytrip.

Jolene, perplexed by Sherry's motives, struggled to decipher the enigma that lay beneath Sherry's resolute facade. Sherry had denied Jolene's request to have some of the other girls join them for the day. Deep within Jolene, a flicker of doubt ignited, casting an ominous shadow over their seemingly innocent gathering. Sherry had purposefully distanced herself from the other girls in their employ, unwilling to forge any connections that might solidify the grim reality of their circumstances. The knowledge of their involvement in the despicable underworld of human trafficking was a burden she didn't want to be tormented by.

Jolene's mind swirled with a maelstrom of thoughts as she endured the unwanted advances and engaged in carnal encounters with the assorted clients at the parties. In the depths of her despair, she sought peace in the refuge of her mind. It was a place where she could shield herself from the harsh realities that plagued her existence. She would retreat, severing all emotional connections to the grim circumstances that unfolded around her. It was the sole method by which she could maintain her sanity. She lay there, her gaze fixed upon the ceiling, lost in the labyrinth of her own ruminations. In the recesses of her consciousness, she found tranquillity, a respite from the cruel reality of her violated form. Though her body was being mercilessly ravaged, her mind remained an impregnable fortress, forever her own.

CHAPTER 24: The birthday.

On Jolene's fourteenth birthday, she fought tooth and nail to suppress her mounting concerns for Tye. Deep within the recesses of her gut, a foreboding sensation gnawed at her, threatening to consume her every thought. Yet, she vowed to orchestrate a day of unparalleled joy for her younger sister, Alice. Her thoughts, like fragile whispers in the wind, would be forced to retreat into the shadows of her mind.

With a steely resolve, she contemplated seeking Sherry's assistance in unearthing Tye's whereabouts. She would have to tread cautiously to avoid arousing Alice's suspicions. With a calculated glance, she observed Alice, captivated by the farm inhabitants that roamed the vast fields. It was the perfect opportunity to engage in a conversation with Sherry. For Alice the farm, was a sanctuary where her true happiness lay hidden amidst the rolling fields. There was only one other place where her spirit soared, where her creativity blossomed. In the realm of dressmaking, where she breathed life into her mother's old singer sewing machine, weaving threads of passion and artistry into every stitch.

Jolene was determined to uncover the truth behind Sherry's decision to exclude certain girls from joining them. The perplexing puzzle of Sherry's motives gnawed at Jolene's curiosity, compelling her to delve deeper into her friend's stance. "I need your help," Jolene said to Sherry, as Alice was distracted in the goat barn." Tye has gone missing. He never returned home after visiting family in the country, do you think you could ask a couple of the drivers and Shady why he hasn't returned? Only I have a horrible feeling." Sherry scowled as she responded, "Why didn't you tell me sooner child? Of course, I'll call my brother." Jolene moved closer to hug her, relieved that she now had an ally. "There's one more question I have for you, why didn't you want the other girls to join us today, only, Maria allowed it?" Jolene looked at Sherry expectantly, she adored her, she was like a guardian angel to her, but Jolene still missed Maria. "If I'm honest, the more I know, the less I want to know about the family business, if the girls were here and talked about the parties, it would make it too real for me, so I'm sorry child, but I just can't, I don't think I will ever be as strong as you are?" Jolene felt a tinge of sadness at Sherry's words, but at least she now understood her reasoning.

As the sun dipped below the horizon, casting long shadows across the sprawling farm, Sherry, and the girls, bid farewell to the rustic charm of the countryside. Their hearts filled with the memories of a day well spent, they made their journey home. Where dinner awaited them in the oven. Sherry's nerves were taut, her senses heightened, mirroring the unease that gripped the girls.

The impending return of Otis loomed over them like a dark cloud. His company was shunned by all, each one of them avoiding his presence whenever possible. A palpable air of disdain hung heavy in the room, as their collective loathing for him simmered just beneath the surface. The very essence of his being, his beliefs, and his abhorrent treatment of women had become a repugnant stain upon their souls. Yet, they were all bound by an unspoken decree, forced to wear masks of false adoration, whenever he graced them with his presence. Sherry's intentions were pure, her heart filled with compassion for the girls she had vowed to protect.

Sherry was naive, she didn't know that a sinister force lurked in the shadows, threatening to shatter her noble purpose. Otis, a man of dubious character, had set his sights on Sherry. With each passing day, his advances grew bolder, his intentions more sinister. He was relentless in his pursuit, making it increasingly arduous for Sherry to evade his clutches. Sherry fought to maintain her composure in the face of this relentless predator. She possessed a sharp intellect, yet deep down, she harboured an unsettling truth: she was no match for Otis.

The sisters moved with a sense of purpose in the dimly lit kitchen. Their delicate hands deftly sliced and diced, the rhythmic clatter of knives echoing through the air. The tantalising aroma of spices and simmering sauces wafted through the room, filling it with the tantalising smell of home cooking. Just as the table was being adorned with fine China and gleaming silverware, the door swung open, revealing two figures. Otis, with his dishevelled hair and wild eyes, exuded an aura of madness that surpassed his usual eccentricity.

Sherry, ever observant, couldn't help but notice the peculiar change in her brother, Shady. His once vibrant complexion had turned ashen, as if drained of life itself, and lines etched across his face, as if the weight of the world had suddenly descended upon him. It was as if the passage of a single night had aged him beyond measure. He stood there, a mere shadow of the man he once was. The light that once danced in his eyes had vanished, leaving behind a void of desolation. His once infectious smile, now a distant memory, had been replaced by an eerie absence.

Otis couldn't help but reveal a sinister smile. With a sneer that dripped with malevolence, "Tye," he began, his voice laced with a twisted satisfaction, "shall no longer be your driver, Jolene. He found himself entangled with the wrong crowd, and a little bird whispered in my ear that he met his untimely demise last night." His laughter, devoid of any remorse, echoed through the room, chilling the very air they breathed. Jolene's eyes, like a stormy sea, brimmed with tears, cascading down her exquisite countenance. The force of her emotions sent the table into a dizzying whirl, threatening to unleash the tumbling dishes. With a heart heavy with anguish, she fled to the sanctuary of her bedroom, her desperate cries echoing through the hollow corridors of her soul.

With her dinner consumed, Alice ascended the staircase in haste, her footsteps echoing through the dimly lit hallway. She sought the company of her sister, within the confines of their shared sanctuary. Before departing, she bestowed a tender kiss upon the cheek of Otis, her affectionate gesture accompanied by a whispered goodnight. With a bitter taste lingering on her lips, she begrudgingly pressed them against him, feigning affection as she uttered the word "dad." Jolene had made her promise to perform this charade.

The dinner lay before her, an unwanted feast that she had no appetite for. She wanted to run after her sister. Jolene needed her. But she dared not abandon her seat, for the mere thought of Otis unleashing his wrath on the room made her compliant. Uncle Shady, appeared visibly tormented. The weight of time had etched deep lines upon his weathered face, betraying the toll that recent events had taken on his soul. Alice, ever perceptive, couldn't help but notice the subtle transformation in her uncle's countenance.

A morbid curiosity engulfed her, for she suspected that Otis, had made him an unwitting accomplice to the heinous crime that had claimed Tye's life. A wave of despair washed over her, her heart sinking like a stone in her chest. There, before her very eyes, was Jolene, on her knees, her voice pleading with the heavens above, beseeching God himself to eradicate Otis from existence. "Oh Alice," Jolene gasped, her voice trembling with anguish, tears streaming down her face, and her nose running uncontrollably. "He's done it. He's killed him." Her eyes darted nervously, searching for any sign of the truth she so desperately sought. "He has murdered Tye."

Alice extended an embroidered handkerchief to Jolene, a silent offering amidst the suffocating tension. With a tender embrace, she enveloped her sister, knowing deep down that her options were tragically limited. Tears cascaded down their faces, mingling with the weight of their shared anguish. Their sobs echoed, a haunting melody. In the depths of their despair, they turned to prayer, their whispered pleas rising like smoke, vanishing into the ether.

Shady savoured the remainder of his dinner, the taste of betrayal lingering on his tongue. With a heavy heart, he bid his sister Sherry farewell, planting a bittersweet kiss upon her cheek. Exhaustion weighed upon him like an anchor, dragging him towards the comfort of his bed. Beneath his weariness, a tempest of emotions raged within him. Otis, once a trusted ally, had become a venomous snake in his eyes. The role he played in Tye's demise had ignited a seething hatred, one that Shady concealed with practised finesse.

He needed a break from the ever-present shadow of Otis. Otis had become unbearable, driving him to seek some peace in separation. He needed a moment of clarity, a chance to delve into his thoughts and strategize his next steps. The weight of the world pressed upon him as he grappled with the daunting task of concocting a plausible tale to relay to Tye's father, a man with whom he shared a bond forged over countless years. He was so fatigued, his eyes failed to detect the concealed terror etched upon Sherry's countenance.

CHAPTER 25: Violation.

The moment Shady departed, Otis succumbed to the allure of intoxication, drowning his thoughts in copious amounts of liquor, and indulging in the hazy embrace of his illicit stash of marijuana. Sherry, against the nagging voice of caution in her mind, mustered the courage to speak up. Her voice, laced with a hint of trepidation, cut through the heavy silence that enveloped the room. "Tell me the truth, Otis," she implored, her eyes fixed on his face. "You killed that boy, didn't you?" Otis stared at her with a cold, calculating gaze, his eyes betraying nothing but a hint of amusement. The dimly lit room seemed to shrink around them, the air thick with tension. She could feel the weight of his silence, a heavy cloak of uncertainty that hung between them. "Answer me, Otis," Sherry demanded.

In a sudden burst of chaos, the room transformed into a battleground. Tables and chairs were hurled through the air, colliding with reckless abandon. The delicate China, once poised with elegance, shattered upon impact, its fragments scattered across the floor. Amidst the wreckage, the remnants of uneaten food lay strewn on the floor and walls. In a chilling display of brutality, Otis seized Sherry by a handful of her lustrous locks, his grip unyielding.

With a malevolence that knew no bounds, he unleashed a torrent of merciless blows upon her defenceless form, each strike a testament to his sadistic nature. As her cries for mercy fell upon deaf ears, he callously forced her down onto the cold, unforgiving floor. In a grotesque act of violation, Otis tore at the delicate fabric that shielded Sherry's modesty, his actions driven by a depravity that defied comprehension. The sanctity of her being shattered, he subjected her to a harrowing ordeal, an unspeakable violation that left her soul scarred and her body broken. His depravity knew no limits as he subjected her to unspeakable acts of sodomy, further cementing his status as a monster in human form. The assault endured, stretching out into an eternity of torment. Otis, a malevolent force, ravaged her very essence, his venomous words dripping from his lips. Her piercing screams echoed through the room, a desperate plea for salvation.

With every ounce of strength she possessed, she valiantly struggled against the sinister figure that loomed over her. But her efforts were in vain, mere flickers of resistance against an unstoppable force. Otis, consumed by a seething rage, harboured a sinister plan to impart a lesson upon her. How audacious of her to reject his advances, as if she held some elevated status above him. This insolent woman had clearly overestimated her own worth, oblivious to his true nature. He savagely tore apart every garment that adorned her frame, leaving her exposed and vulnerable. The attack carried on for hours, until Otis was finally spent, he had filled her up with his seed, and he had enjoyed every thrust and every abusive word.

The aftermath of his brutal assault left her bruised and battered, her once flawless complexion now marred by crimson stains. Tremors wracked her fragile form as she dragged herself to a corner of the kitchen, her body curled protectively around itself, a feeble attempt to shield her shattered spirit from further harm. All of a sudden, he stood up and pissed on her, a contemptuous act that dripped with disdain. With a smug satisfaction etched upon his face, he turned on his heel and strode out of the house, leaving her broken body and soul to deal with the harrowing ordeal he had just put her through.

As the sun's rays gently caressed the room, Alice and Jolene slowly emerged from their slumber. Yet, instead of the usual symphony of clattering pots and pans that accompanied the dawn, an eerie silence enveloped the air. Sherry, their ever-reliable caretaker, was conspicuously absent from her usual post in the kitchen, where she would diligently prepare their morning breakfast.

The house stood in an unsettling stillness. Not a sound dared to escape its walls. Jolene, with her bloodshot eyes, cautiously stepped into the kitchen, her senses overwhelmed by the chaotic scene that unfolded before her. Broken plates and shattered glass littered the floor, mingling with the crimson stains of a violent struggle. The air was heavy with the metallic scent of blood, intermingled with the pungent aroma of spoiled food. Fear coursed through her veins, gripping her heart with an icy hand.

Her eyes darted around the room, searching for any sign of danger. With every creak of the floorboards, her eyes widened in horror. Alice stood frozen, her gaze locked with Jolene's as both girls shared a moment of disbelief. In the dimly lit corner, a chilling sight awaited them - the trembling form of Sherry, her body exposed and shattered, a haunting tableau of violence. Jolene, with a sense of urgency, approached Alice, beseeching her to retrieve Sherry's dressing gown. In that fateful moment, Sherry succumbed to her overwhelming emotions, her tear-stained face resembling a cascading waterfall.

Deep within her tortured soul, she unleashed a silent scream, berating herself for her paralysing fear and incapacitating pain, which had rendered her defenceless and in no fit state to clean away any evidence of the night's events. She should have hidden it from the girls who had stumbled upon her in this pitiful condition. Sherry found herself trapped, by a chilling terror that gripped her soul.

The merciless hands of fate had conspired against her, as Otis, unleashed a storm of violence upon her fragile form. With a kitchen knife as his weapon of choice, he callously carved deep wounds into her flesh, each cut a testament, to the brutality of the attack that unfolded before her very eyes. His eyes fixated on the crimson spectacle, a twisted pleasure emanating from within.

The vessel before him bore the marks of his savagery, a macabre canvas adorned with merciless slashes. Her once flawless countenance had been marred by his merciless blade, leaving behind a grotesque visage that bore no resemblance to the beauty she once possessed. Jolene sprang into action, her movements swift and purposeful. With a frightened look in her eyes, she swiftly placed a kettle on the stove, its flames dancing beneath it.

Her voice echoed through the room, commanding Alice to fetch a bowl, towels and the antiseptic bottles that had been left behind by the doctor. The urgency in her tone was palpable, as if time itself was conspiring against them. With a trembling hand, she hoisted Sherry upright, concealing the fear that threatened to swamp her. This scene was all too familiar, reminiscent of a time when her mother still drew breath. Never in her darkest imaginings did she envision Otis, inflicting such horrors on poor Sherry.

CHAPTER 26: Gone.

"M<small>EMORIES</small>"

'Sherry was raped and then butchered by him. She isn't even his wife. I'm petrified that Sherry may disappear and leave us to fend for ourselves. Then there wouldn't be anyone to look after us. I can't say that I blame her. She has become a husk of her former self, completely unrecognisable. She has severe scars from that night. Please, God, take the life of that vile monster. Sherry asked us not to tell Shady, that Otis did this too her fearing he would murder him, then spend his life in prison. Instead, she told him that she had been robbed, that it happened on the street. Shady will never know the full extent of her suffering since she covers up her wounds with makeup and clothing. Not that he has shown any enthusiasm as of late; rather, he appears distracted and even sad. I haven't had much time to grieve over Tye's passing, but I do believe that Otis would have come for me as well. If he had realised how much we loved each other. At the very least, I should be thankful for that small mercy. I don't buy Shady's story that Tye was slain because he was cooperating with the cops. Surely that's not the case. This existence has taught me to function without showing emotional attachments, but I miss him so much it hurts. Otis prevents any of us from showing any feelings. If he knows we care, he'll make our suffering even worse.'

Sherry, with her wounds still fresh, bided her time. Patiently awaiting the day when she would finally be able to depart for Trinidad. She despised the very essence of her being. In the presence of Otis, she would involuntarily diminish, as if overrun by an invisible force that emanated from his mere presence. She trembled in fear, her heart pounding like a drum in her chest.

He had spared her from his gruesome acts this time, refraining from slicing her flesh. Yet, the scars of his sadistic nature still haunted her, rendering her powerless to resist his perverse desires. He whispered into her ear with a venomous hiss, asserting his dominion over her, declaring her as his possession, subject to his every whim. Indifferent to her icy stillness, he remained unperturbed. Her lack of response to his advances failed to faze him, as did her refusal to return his kisses.

For Otis, it was never about affection; it was always about dominance and control. She despised the nocturnal visits of his, when he would grace her presence, savouring every moment of her anguish, prolonging her torment for endless hours. Her once radiant smile had become a mere shadow of its former self, a casualty of the burdens she carried. The weight of her troubles had etched deep lines of sorrow upon her face, leaving little room for joy to find its way through. Each passing day, her smile grew feebler, as if it were a fragile thread, barely holding on to her shattered spirit.

The world had dealt her a cruel hand, and the toll it had taken, was evident in the weariness that clouded her eyes. The only path to restoration lay in escaping this living nightmare, leaving it in the dust of her past. In her heart, she yearned to rescue the innocent sisters, from the clutches of a destiny more sinister than the grave itself. Alas, she was all too aware that Otis, a relentless predator, would pursue them relentlessly, akin to a rabid hound chasing its prey across the vast expanse of the world. Her spirit, once fierce and indomitable, had been drained of its last ounce of strength, leaving her bereft.

The formidable fortress of airport security stood as an impenetrable barrier. The indomitable force of authority would surely deny her passage, forbidding her from whisking away the innocent girls to safety. In her tormented soul, she confronted the most harrowing choice of her existence. The weight of her decision bore down upon her, threatening to shatter her sanity. Yet, she knew that in order to preserve her tenuous grip on reality, she had no choice but to sever all ties with Otis. She needed to flee to her homeland. And flee she would.

Her heart pounded in her chest as she contemplated the daunting task of revealing the truth to the girls. The weight of the impending confession threatening to overwhelm her. Sherry knew deep down that it was a necessary evil, a moral obligation she could not evade. The shadows of guilt loomed over her, casting a sinister pallor upon her conscience. With a heavy sigh, she steeled herself, determined to face the consequences of her actions.

From the bottom of the staircase, Sherry's voice reverberated through the house, "Girls, please come downstairs," she called out. In a matter of mere minutes, the rhythmic thud of their footsteps could be heard growing louder with each passing second. In an attempt to cushion the impact, she had prepared a steaming pot of tea and an array of delectable pastries.

The table, adorned with these tempting treats, awaited the ravenous appetites of the girls. Otis and Shady were on another trip to Nottingham, providing Sherry and the girls with a much-needed space from Otis's evil character. Jolene and Alice glided into the kitchen, their eyes fixated on the tantalising display of cakes before them.

Jolene, with her piercing gaze and a voice as smooth as silk, was the first to break the silence. "Looks yummy," she uttered, as her gaze locked with Sherry's. "But you shouldn't be overexerting yourself? You're not fully healed.". Sherry, burdened by the weight of her guilt, was the first to look away. The three figures stood in a triangular formation, their faces etched with worry and uncertainty. "I need to speak with you both," her voice quivered, betraying a sense of desperation. "I... I... I'm leaving tonight, my flights booked. I'm going home." The room fell silent, the gravity of the situation sinking in. Sherry's eyes darted nervously, searching for a glimmer of understanding in the eyes of the girls. But all she found was a mixture of surprise and concern. The decision had been made, the die cast." I'm afraid I can't stay here any longer girls," she murmured with a heavy heart. "Please forgive me." Tears streamed down her face as she uttered those words, her voice full of anguish and despair. In a tender display of solidarity, Jolene and Alice approached her, their eyes filled with unspoken understanding.

As they drew closer, their arms enveloped her in a collective embrace, their bodies intertwining in a poignant moment of shared grief. Tears cascaded down their cheeks, mingling with the raw emotions that coursed through their veins. The trio found a shared vulnerability, their tears becoming a testament to the unbreakable bond that united them.

PUSHING THEM AWAY, Sherry propelled the girls backward, their tear-stained faces drained of any remaining moisture." I must bid you adieu, my girls. I would love to take you away from this place. Please forgive me, for even if you possessed the necessary travel documents, the ever-vigilant airport security would prevent me leaving with you. As for your stepfather..." her voice trailed off, she dared not utter the full extent of her thoughts.

The truth was already hanging in the air, a palpable presence that threatened them all. Alice stood with a determined look in her eyes. "Otis would hunt us down to the ends of the earth," she whispered. Her words were heavy, with an undeniable finality that engulfed the room. The weight of her statement settled upon each person present, their collective breaths held captive by the gravity of her words.

In that moment, Jolene's voice quivered as she uttered the words, "He is still hurting you, isn't he?" Sherry could only manage a nod, her eyes betraying the fear that consumed her. The weight of the truth threatened to spill from her quivering mouth, but she knew that surrendering to its release would only lead to another devastating breakdown. Alice's hunger got the better of her, a constant companion that grew insistent in moments of sadness. And so, with a mixture of resignation and longing, she took a bite of a Victoria sponge, savouring the bittersweet taste that offered temporary reprieve to her troubled soul.

Jolene's voice was but a hushed murmur, "We won't see you again, will we?" her words dripping with an air of finality. A solitary teardrop fell down Sherry's cheekbone. With a voice laced with sorrow, she mustered the strength to respond, "No, my dear child, I don't think you will." With a graceful flourish, she gathered her belongings, a sense of purpose emanating from her every move. As she bid farewell to each girl, her lips pressed against their cheeks in a tender manner. Sherry strode towards the awaiting taxi, her heart breaking but she *never looked back.*

"Jolene, what are we going to do now that Sherry's gone too?" Alice asked quietly as she and Jolene sobbed in the kitchen. Jolene replied softly, "I really don't know sis, Sherry had to escape, otherwise he would have probably killed her too." Jolene's face was pale and sad, and she had black circles under her eyes from all the crying she had done in her short life. Otis was hell-bent on destroying everything that made their lives worth living, her thoughts were all over the place due to her grief, and she had a sinking feeling in her stomach that things were only going to get worse. The only person left now who seemed to care about her and Alice, was Shady, and she didn't have much faith in him. He seemed to have shut himself off from everyone after Maria's death.

CHAPTER 27: No allies.

"MEMORIES"

'Sherry abandoned us and left us to fend for ourselves against Otis. I just know that everything is going to go horribly wrong. I'm worried for the girls that work for us, and I'm worried for myself and Alice. Otis repeatedly attacked Sherry, I don't know why. I really don't understand. Now that we are defenceless, I fear that Otis will come for me and Alice. He will hurt us because nobody else is in his way. I'm frightened because I made a promise to Alice, who will turn twelve in a matter of weeks, and I'm not sure I can keep it. Will he pressure her into having sex with clients? How do I leave Alice alone at night when I have to do the parties. I don't know what to do; I made a promise to her and now I'm afraid I won't be able to keep it. Someone, please help us,'

Jolene was acutely aware that her options were limited, she was trapped by Otis. The thought of defying him and staying home to care for Alice was nothing more than a fleeting fantasy, that would surely be met with dire consequences. The parties, with their sinister allure and hidden agendas, beckoned her into a world of darkness and deceit. Jolene's heart sank as she resigned herself to the inevitable, knowing that her fate was sealed by the merciless hands of her captor. Jolene had contemplated the idea of taking Alice with her, leaving her in the care of her drivers, but they had all adamantly declined. In the early hours, she would return from the parties. Her steps as silent as a whisper, she would tiptoe into Alice's bedroom. She would slip into the bed beside her, with a touch as gentle as a feather brushing against skin. Two weeks had passed since Sherry's abrupt departure, leaving a void in the household. Jolene, ever resilient, had seamlessly slipped into the role of the nurturing figure once again. Night after night, she diligently prepared sumptuous meals for Otis.

The weight of her worries lifted when Shady would join them for meals too. Shady had remained tight-lipped, refusing to divulge any details about, Tye or Sherry. Yet, Jolene, with her keen intuition, sensed the heavy burden of guilt that plagued him. Otis kept a watchful eye on Shady, as if he knew something the rest of the household didn't. In Jolene's heart, a flicker of hope emerged. She dared to believe that Shady, had been trying to keep Otis at bay, ensuring his absence from the home whilst Jolene was at work.

Jolene arrived home and was weary, from yet another night's toil, amidst the raucous revelry of the house party. The relentless demands of her occupation had taken a toll on her fragile physique. Getting into bed, she gave her sister a tender peck on her cheek, a familiar routine. Nestling herself beside the comforting warmth of her sibling's form, sliding her arm under the pillow. A curious sensation tingled through her fingertips, hinting at the presence of something concealed. A single envelope lay there, its contents bulging. With trembling hands, Jolene gingerly opened the envelope, revealing a substantial sum of money. A letter, neatly folded, accompanied the stack of notes. Its words, carefully penned,

"Tye would want you to have this money. It was a token of his devotion, with it his dreams he nurtured for your shared destiny. I hope this will aid your predicament. My prayers shall forever be with you." Yours faithfully, Tye's father."

Jolene's eyes widened in disbelief as they fixated upon the staggering sum of money before her. In the dead of night, she emerged from the bed, her movements silent. With one graceful step, she approached the bed's edge, her eyes focussed on the loose floorboard nestled in the dimly lit corner of the room. With trembling hands, she carefully concealed the envelope and its precious contents within the concealed abyss. The darkness swallowed her secrets whole, as she restored the floorboard to its rightful place, erasing any trace of her activities. Silent tears traced a path of sorrow on her hauntingly beautiful face. With a heavy heart, she got back into bed, seeking the comforting presence of her beloved sister.

A torrent of questions flooded her mind, swirling like a tempest in the dead of night. With each query, a sharp blade pierced her thoughts with relentless precision. Who? When? How? The weariness that had once consumed her had now dissipated, leaving no trace of its existence. Had Shady put the envelope there?

Jolene, her mind full of confusion, struggled to unravel the tangled threads of her reality. She was no match for the relentless grip of exhaustion that tightened its hold, overpowering her valiant efforts. With a weary sigh, she succumbed to the seductive embrace of sleep, surrendering herself to her dreams. The following morning, Jolene's spirits soared as she diligently prepared breakfast for Alice. As the door swung open, Otis sauntered into the room, his presence commanding attention, with Shady, following closely behind. Taking their places at the kitchen table, they awaited the arrival of a full English breakfast.

Once seated, they engaged in a conversation that glided on the edge of legality. Otis was complaining about the burden that had befallen him - the solitary task of tending to the books. Shady, concealed his thoughts. Trying desperately to avoid a confrontation he knew he would lose.

Meanwhile, Jolene could no longer contain the burning question that had haunted her for what seemed like an eternity. In a moment of unguarded vulnerability, she abruptly blurted out, " Shady, have you had any word from Sherry? please tell her we miss her." Shady's countenance transformed, his features assuming a hardened facade as a cynical sneer etched across his face, his eyes pierced through Otis's very soul. "Yes," he replied with a voice as smooth as whisky, "I have spoken to her. She, misses you too." Otis, a rugged figure with a hardened gaze, defiantly flapped his arms in the air, his voice laced with a hint of danger. "Listen mate," he growled, his words dripping with suspicion, "if you've got something to say, come straight out and say it." They locked eyes, a silent understanding passing between them. Jolene's heart pounded in her chest as she silently berated herself for succumbing to such a foolish mistake.

CHAPTER 28: Destroyer.

Shady's appetite waned as he stared at the sumptuous breakfast spread before him. Across the table, Alice mirrored his every action, her eyes fixed on him with an unsettling intensity. The air thickened with an unspoken tension as they both toyed with their food, their movements synchronised, their expressions identical. The room fell silent, broken only by the sound of Otis's exaggerated slurps as he savoured his coffee.

Jolene's eyes, sharp as a hawk's, remained fixed on Shady and Alice, as if she were dissecting their every move with surgical precision. Jolene had developed a habit of abstaining from joining the others for breakfast. This behaviour had become a constant, ever since the departure of Sherry. In her eyes it was the only thing she had control over. However, it was not only Sherry's absence that had caused this change in Jolene's routine.

The tragic demise of Tye had also resulted in a drastic decline of her appetite. Jolene was now barely consuming enough sustenance to sustain her fragile existence. A subtle, mischievous smile adorned her face, a tell-tale sign of her amusement, as she observed the duo engaged in a captivating game of mimicry at the table. Alice, may the heavens bless her soul, possessed an innate talent for lifting the spirits of those around her.

Shady couldn't help but crack a fleeting smile in response to Alice's antics. With a satisfied gluttony, Otis devoured his meal, crumbs sprinkling down his chin like a trail of evidence. Seizing a slice of toast, he spread it with a generous layer of tangy marmalade. As he sank his teeth into the delectable concoction, a malevolent glint became apparent in his eyes.

With calculated precision, Otis prepared to unleash a revelation, shattering the fragile peace. "I believe it's high time, I make my presence known to the girls who are earning me money at the party houses". His words, dripped with menace, like a carefully orchestrated chess move, hinting at his sinister intentions. Jolene's countenance betrayed her inner turmoil, her eyes wide with fear. "Please, Otis," she pleaded, her voice quivering, "do not scare the girls." In a moment of unbridled fury, Otis, consumed by a tempestuous rage, unleashed a vicious slap on Jolene's delicate face. The force of the blow propelled her frail form towards the unforgiving ground, where she collided with a resounding thud that echoed ominously within the confines of the kitchen. Leaning menacingly over her, he bellowed with a finger thrust accusingly in her direction, "You, dare speak to me like that. Those girls, they are mine, under my command, and I shall exercise my dominion over them as I damn well please. Do you hear me?" It was a threat, a chilling reminder of just how vicious Otis could be. Each person present felt the weight of it, their hearts pounding in unison, their eyes darting nervously from one to another. They all knew, deep down, that this was no idle remark. It was a warning, he had set his sights on marking his territory. His mind, a dark abyss of sinister thoughts, was consumed by a single objective, to strike fear into the hearts of the girls who dared to cross his path. In his eyes this was the only means to establish an ironclad grip on his workforce. Not once did it occur to him that Jolene had been deftly handling the situation all by herself, under his very nose.

    In the darkness of the night, Otis and Shady embarked on their journey, venturing into the depths of debauchery. As they traversed the maze, of party houses, a shadow of guilt cast itself upon Shady's soul. His eyes averted, he found himself confronted by a bevy of young girls, their provocative propositions were like a punch to his core. Otis, ever the opportunist, had eagerly accepted every single offer that came his way, leaving poor Shady to fend for himself. Tears streamed down the faces of a few young girls as they emerged from the confines of the bedrooms, their encounters with Otis having left them emotionally shattered. They found themselves unaccustomed to his forceful demeanour, as he subjected them to his brutal touch during their intimate liaisons.

    After witnessing the gruesome aftermath of Otis's heinous acts upon the first of his many innocent victims, Shady knew all too well that it was in his best interest to remain outside, seeking company of the vigilant doorman, instead. He lacked the courage to confront Otis. Jolene found herself in the heart of one of the party houses.

The air was thick with anticipation, as she navigated through a sea of revellers. In the chaos, her phone buzzed incessantly, each message a cryptic missive from the girls who held sway over her thoughts. Otis had already caused chaos. His malevolence knew no bounds, as evidenced by the chilling incident where he brandished a knife against one girl.

He had threatened to sever her tongue, all because she made the mistake of catching his manhood with her teeth. Jolene's heart sank, a wave of despair washing over her. There, in the depths of her soul, she knew that her options had dwindled to nothingness. Word travelled with the swiftness of a raging inferno, whispering its secrets to Jolene's ears. A handful of the girls were so terrified by Otis, that they had threatened to jump ship. She found it difficult to blame them, for their actions were driven by a primal instinct for self-preservation. Deep within her heart, she dreaded the possibility of Otis, with his twisted psyche, relentlessly pursuing them, inflicting unimaginable pain or, worse yet, snuffing out their lives for the audacity of leaving him behind. All she could do was watch in despair as the fruits of her labour began to crumble like a house of cards.

The blood, sweat, and tears she had poured into her endeavours were now evaporating into thin air, leaving behind only a bitter taste of dread. The party houses would be rendered useless with no girls to frequent them. Otis was a fool, he seemed determined to dismantle the very foundations of Jolene's arduously crafted empire. Deep within the recesses of her soul, she always knew he would destroy everything.

CHAPTER 29: Help us.

Shady's nerves were stretched thin, his composure teetering on the edge of collapse. Otis, with his imposing presence, had a way of instilling a bone-chilling fear into his employees. One by one, the girls vanished into thin air, lost to the world without a trace. Fate dealt him a cruel hand, compelling him to relinquish the tenancies and sever ties with his loyal doormen and drivers.

Otis didn't seem to care about his crumbling empire, a madness had taken hold. Once revered for his cunning intellect and shrewd business acumen, Otis had descended into depravity. No longer content with the power he wielded, Otis now sought to exert control over the very souls of those who toiled under his command.

Otis revelled in his newfound authority. His twisted mind concocted a wicked game, of manipulation and seduction. He demanded that every girl in his employ endure his lascivious advances, disguised as lessons in the art of their trade. Under the guise of mentorship, Otis preyed upon the vulnerability of his female subordinates.

Their dreams and aspirations, once kindled by the promise of professional growth, were now smothered by the suffocating grip of his perverse desires. Each encounter, a calculated move in his sinister game, left a trail of shattered innocence and broken spirits in its wake. The premise he clung to was that he was doing them a favour, a twisted service.

In the ensuing weeks, he embarked upon a relentless quest, he sought out every party Jolene had organised. With a calculated charm, he skillfully manipulated the unsuspecting females. Through whispered words and beguiling gestures, he coerced them and threatened them, into surrendering their bodies and souls to him. In the throes of passion's embrace, he revelled in the dangerous game, heedless of the consequences that loomed ominously. He sought to demean and harm the girls. He sought to terrify them, to own them, to possess them entirely.

He would not allow them to use condoms, the mere suggestion earning them a scar on their necks. Evil incarnate, he unleashed his wrath upon a couple of unsuspecting girls who dared to defy his unwelcome advances. The weight of it all bore down heavily on Jolene's shoulders. They were her friends and she had let them down. She could no longer keep them safe. The guilt she felt was insurmountable.

Night after night, she found herself at the party houses, with not enough girls to keep the clients occupied. Instead, she was met with a disheartening reality. One or two girls would be there if she was lucky, spreading themselves thinly. They had no other choice but to cater to the insatiable desires of the customers. The situation pushed the remaining girls to their limits, they were at breaking point. Shady found himself trapped, his every move under Otis's relentless scrutiny. With no escape in sight, he was left with no choice but to employ the services of a discreet messenger, a runner who would carry his messages to Jolene.

"THE MESSAGES"

'He is hellbent on wrecking everything, it's like a madness has taken over him. He has changed doormen and drivers for more violent types without informing me. This week alone I have had to let go of twelve party houses, because the girls are a no show. I know we are losing money hand over fist, but he doesn't seem to care. All he wants to do is destroy everything you have worked hard for. The shipments up country is all that is keeping us afloat right now. I think he is running it into the ground on purpose, don't be surprised if he closes shop permanently. I'm sorry I can't be there for you both, he watches my every move'.

JOLENE FOUND HERSELF on the edge of exhaustion, her body aching for sustenance that she stubbornly denied it. The relentless demands of her profession forced her to accept more clients, each party draining her further. Weakness consumed her, rendering her motionless, a prisoner of her own fear. In Otis's transformation, a monster had taken hold, he became colder and more calculated. Every mealtime, he would unleash his wrath upon her, hurling the plates of food at her, as if they were weapons of destruction. The remnants of which he would smear across her delicate features, in a grotesque display of power and control. She would be left with no choice but to bow to his sadistic demands, dutifully scrubbing away the leftovers from the floor. These days he was like a deranged psychopath. His very essence seemed as if he were possessed by a demon. She had always sensed a darkness within him, that lurked beneath his charming facade. But what she was about to discover would shatter her perception of him entirely.

It was a revelation that would plunge her into the depths of a sinister world she never knew existed. Her heart raced, pounding against her chest like a caged bird desperate for freedom. The fear that gripped her was palpable, she wasn't alone in her terror. Alice, too, felt the icy grip of fear tighten around her, her eyes wide with trepidation. In the depths of their shared dread, they found themselves trapped. There was no reprieve, no sanctuary to be found. Jolene's heart raced as she anticipated his return. She was all too aware of his capricious temperament, a volatile storm that could unleash its fury without warning or reason. Jolene had cooked his favourite meal with every intention of appeasing his volatile temperament. Poor Alice rarely spoke anymore, Jolene's intuition proved astute as she correctly surmised that the purpose behind it all was to shield herself from Otis's noxious eruptions of anger. Jolene and Alice were in the midst of arranging the cutlery on the table, their delicate hands moving with precision, when the door swung open, revealing Otis. He strode in, flanked by two colossal men. Jolene's heart skipped a beat, a fleeting moment of panic coursing through her veins. She hastily suppressed her emotions, realising with a sinking feeling that there wasn't enough food for the unexpected guests. Otis and the two towering figures leered at the two sisters, their eyes filled with hatred and lust. A deep, unsettling sensation stirred within her bowels, a primal instinct warning her of the impending danger. The men, their eyes gleaming with a predatory hunger, fixated on their target as if they were savage beasts stalking their prey in the wilderness. In an instant, a realisation struck Jolene like a bolt of lightning, jolting her senses awake. The men stood before her were not here for dinner.

"THE MESSAGES"

'I'll never forget the looks on those men's faces when they came home with him last night. Alice and I were bound and raped and tortured for hours. Otis sat on a chair in the corner of the room, smoked a joint, and drank spiced rum, all the while laughing. One of the men slapped Alice across the face repeatedly, since she made no attempt to cry out for help, but she still made no sound. Otis gave the men free reign over our bodies so long as they didn't "mark his product," as he put it, and now we're both lost in our own worlds. I feel like such a liar to Alice since I swore this would never happen again. The men smashed our bodies into the crevices of the dirt, and now Alice and I are both so sore. I cannot work the parties tonight. Alice won't even talk to me. I suspect she blames me.' It's my fault, it's all my fault. We need to run away, we need to get far away. But how?'

CHAPTER 30: Forgive me.

"Alice please speak to me," Jolene's voice was trembling with desperation, as she pleaded for her attention. Jolene had promised her something, something of great importance, and now it lay shattered at their feet. The sound of her voice, filled with regret and longing. "I swear, I tried everything to ensure your safety," she confessed, her voice barely audible within the suffocating confines of the room.

In that moment, Alice's gaze fixated upon her beloved sister, her eyes filled with a profound affection that transcended mere words. With a hushed tone, she uttered, "You mustn't blame yourself, I had an inkling that Otis would come for me, when Sherry abandoned us." Her delicate smile quivered, betraying a hint of vulnerability, as she involuntarily flinched, a subtle wince escaping her lips, marred by a cruel split.

Jolene gingerly approached Alice, her eyes filled with compassion, hugging her in a tender embrace. They remained entwined on the edge of the bed. Their countenances bore the unmistakable marks of a violent encounter, their visages marred by the cruel hands of the night's events. The bruises, like dark omens, adorned their faces, evidence to the merciless blows they had endured.

It was not only their faces that bore the scars of their ordeal. A searing pain, akin to the scorching touch of a branding iron, seeped through their beings, nestled between their thighs, a haunting reminder of the horrors they had faced. Today marked a significant occasion in the life of Alice, it was her birthday. Alice, at the tender age of twelve, found herself in a world devoid of celebration. The two sisters, their faces etched with pain, sought out the ritualistic act of purifying their bodies. It was the only thing they could do. Wash away the dirt, wash away their shame.

It had become a familiar routine, a necessary penance they willingly embraced after each harrowing incident that had befallen them. In a hushed tone, Jolene's voice barely audible, she revealed, "I've put a small drop of bleach into the bath, just as I did last time. Mom used to swear by it, do you remember?" Their eyes met, two lost souls adrift in the vast expanse of their own thoughts. "Listen Alice," she whispered, with secrecy. "I have something to show you, something that must remain a secret." With gentle steps, she made her way to the corner of the room, where a loose floorboard awaited her.

As she delicately raised it from the floor, her knees, battered and bruised sank to the unforgiving ground. With bated breath, she retrieved the concealed envelope, her voice trembling as she uttered, "Tye left us this, It's our salvation, our ticket to freedom." The weight of the world pressed upon Alice's weary shoulders, mirroring the thoughts that swirled within her troubled mind. Never had she seen such a large sum of money. Jolene's desperate plea fell on deaf ears, as Alice dismissed her with a resolute tone. "That won't be of any use," she declared, her voice laced with a hint of resignation. "Where would we go, we are too young even with that money." Jolene interrupted, "It's a start." Alice's words struck a chord, resonating with a chilling clarity. Was it all useless?

The question loomed ominously before them: where, could they seek refuge from their relentless tormentor? They were but mere adolescents, far from the age of acquiring a lease or securing employment. The funds they possessed would merely serve as a temporary relief in their precarious circumstances.

"THE MESSAGES"

'I beg your forgiveness. If only I was strong enough, to deal with him for you. Unfortunately, I can only give you a couple of days to get better. Otis and I were lured back to Nottingham. Our latest shipment ended up being a miserable failure. I prayed desperately, hoping that even this small amount of comfort would provide you a momentary reprieve. My stomach is knotted up with worry, about the trip ahead. There is a lot at stake, since I am confident that if our partners found out about his mental instability, they would immediately cut ties with us. No one sane would risk interacting with a man who has lost his mind. His path towards insanity has been a relentless spiral into the depths of derangement. There is no denying the danger and recklessness of his actions. I wish I was capable of doing so much more, for you both. I am so sorry, please forgive me.'

As Otis and Shady approached the Palmers club, the pulsating rhythm of music reverberated through the night, emitting an enchanting spell upon the atmosphere. A throng of eager patrons congregated outside. With a subtle inclination of his head, the doorman silently beckoned them to advance towards the inconspicuous side entrance. Shady exhaled a breath he hadn't realised he was holding, his senses tingling with a newfound relief.

The dimly lit club, once a haunting reminder of the horrors that had unfolded within its walls, now seemed to exude an air of normalcy. Memories of the night they had mercilessly tormented Tye, the hapless victim, and the brazen copper who dared to intervene, still haunted Shady's conscience. The club had been forced to shut down in the aftermath, a necessary consequence of their actions.

But now, as he glanced around, Shady couldn't help but feel a flicker of hope that the past would remain buried, forever concealed beneath the facade of an ordinary establishment. As the burden of his troubles dissipated, he experienced a profound sense of relief. Shady couldn't help but feel a twinge of unease on the drive up as he noticed Otis's uncharacteristic silence throughout the entire journey.

The air was thick with tension, as if a storm was brewing just beneath the surface. Otis, with his brooding demeanour concerned Shady. It was impossible to decipher his thoughts, his intentions, when he wore that inscrutable expression. But Shady knew that silence was not an option. He had to take a risk, to probe Otis's mind, if he hoped to gain any insight into what lay ahead.

With a trembling voice, he mustered the courage to speak, breaking the silence between them. He couldn't be sure of Otis's mood when he was like this. But perhaps, just perhaps, if he engaged him in the art of conversation, he might be able to figure it out. The club was a haven for the lost souls of the city, its atmosphere thick with a potent mix of bodies and smoke. The air itself seemed to writhe with an intoxicating blend of anticipation and danger. In the heart of this den of iniquity, cages adorned the room, each housing a seductive siren whose bare flesh was on display for the rapt audience.

With every twist and turn of their lithe bodies, the gyrating dancers cast a bewitching spell upon the on-looking crowd. Their movements, both graceful and provocative, held the power to captivate even the most jaded of souls. The two men were discreetly guided through the dimly lit establishment, their presence drawing curious glances from the patrons. As they stepped into the smoke-filled room, their eyes were immediately drawn to the imposing figures of the Palmers security team.

Dressed in sharp suits that hugged their muscular frames, these men exuded an air of authority. With a curt nod, one of the guards motioned for them to take a seat, their eyes never leaving the intruders. Before him stood the weathered, ancient wooden office desk, its worn surface reminiscent of a bygone era when it had served as a gambling den.

Both men took a seat, their senses heightened by the absence of the elusive Palmers. A glimmer of hope flickered momentarily when one of the security men extended a gesture of hospitality, offering them a drink. Otis was relishing the burn of his drink as it slid down his throat. As he ignited a joint, its cherry ember releasing a warm hue on his face. With a keen eye, he surveyed his surroundings, absorbing every detail.

He marvelled at the room's impeccable cleanliness, a testament to the meticulousness with which it had been scrubbed. Not a single vestige remained of the grisly bloodshed that had unfolded a month ago, right beneath his very seat. The security guard, a burly figure with a weathered face and a voice as smooth as whisky, extended a glass filled with amber liquid towards them. "The Palmers," he began, "are currently needed elsewhere. They will be late for this meeting."

CHAPTER 31: A rude awakening.

Twenty agonising minutes had slipped away, leaving them none the wiser. The absence of the Palmers continued to hang in the air, putting Otis and Shady on high alert. Shady's nerves were on edge, a creeping unease settling in the pit of his stomach. Otis, his partner in crime, had always been a wild card, but lately, his behaviour had taken a turn for the worst.

Knocking back the rum with a reckless abandon, Otis seemed to be spiralling out of control, as if he were desperately trying to drown his demons in a sea of alcohol. Shady couldn't help but wonder what had pushed Otis to this point, and more importantly, how it would impact their lives. In a sudden twist of fate, a mysterious figure emerged from the office's shadows.

Clad in an elegant ensemble, a white Vivienne Westwood trouser suit, she exuded an air of sophistication. Her age, somewhere in the mid-fifties, was betrayed by her shoulder-length mane of lustrous white hair. Leaving both Otis and Shady in a state of bewilderment, their minds baffled by the turn of events. With a stride that exuded elegant confidence, the lady entered the room, her presence commanding attention. She settled herself gracefully into the plush chair positioned behind the imposing desk. A guard, ever dutiful, swiftly pulled out the chair for her, a subtle gesture of deference that did not go unnoticed.

"Do pardon my lack of introduction, for I have yet to reveal my true identity. Amongst my acquaintances, I am known as Ruby, while my boys address me as Mar. However, in your case, you shall address me as Mrs. Palmer." As the words escaped her lips, a flicker of recognition glided across Otis's face, his eyes narrowing as he struggled to decipher her words.

Shady wanted the ground to swallow him up. There was no way on earth that Otis would willingly work with a woman. Deep down, he sensed that the tempestuous storm brewing within Otis would soon erupt, unleashing a torrent of unbridled fury.

"I must confess that I am the mastermind behind the Palmer empire." Her voice, like a blade slicing through the air, carried a briskness that left no room for idle chatter. It was as if every word she spoke had been carefully chosen, each syllable honed to a razor's edge.

There was no room for ambiguity or hesitation in her tone; it was straight to the point, like a bullet fired from a gun. As she poised herself to resume her speech, a subtle yet commanding gesture escaped her delicate fingertips, catching the attention of the men in the room. In that fleeting moment, an unspoken directive passed through the air, igniting a flurry of swift and calculated movements.

The men sprang into action, their nimble hands expertly binding the two hapless souls before her, rendering them helpless and at her mercy. Once their wrists were bound tightly with coarse rope, she proceeded with her plan. The glint of malevolence in her eyes was concealed behind a mask of fury.

The adhesive grip of masking tape was applied across their mouths, ensuring their voices were silenced, their pleas for mercy stifled. "This is my empire, I rule it with an unyielding grip. Under my watchful eye, I ensure the welfare of all those who work for me. "The words dripped from her lips like venom. Her eyes, cold and steely blue, scanned the room, as if searching for any signs of resistance. "Especially the young girls in my employ," her voice a chilling warning that would ensure the strongest of men would buckle. In that moment, she lit a cigarette inhaling deeply.

With a voice as smooth as silk and eyes that held a thousand untold stories, she spoke with an air of authority. "I, my friend," she uttered "do not deal with certain types of people. You see there exists a breed of individuals who thrive on deceit, thievery, and inflicting pain. Amongst them, a sinister faction emerges, distinguished by their despicable predilection for preying upon innocent little girls." As the words escaped her lips, a chilling silence fell upon the room. The blood seemed to drain from Otis's face, leaving behind a ghostly pallor that betrayed his inner turmoil. Shady, defeated, and despondent, bowed his head in resignation, his gaze fixated on the floor.

"Now, though you may not be in my employ, but our intricate business dealings implicate you, in tarnishing our esteemed standing. Do you comprehend the gravity of my words? With a flourish, she raised her delicate hands, commanding her loyal henchmen with a subtle yet powerful gesture. In a chilling display of calculated menace, a pair of shadowy figures emerged from the depths of the room, their eyes gleaming with a sinister intent.

With a swift and practised motion, they retrieved hunting knives concealed within their trousers. Meanwhile, two additional guard's advanced towards Otis, their purpose clear as they extended two fingers on each hand, ready to seize him in a vice-like grip. The guards surrounded him. Otis, fought against the iron grip of his shackles, his muscles straining with desperation. His efforts proved futile, as the restraints held him captive.

As the blade made its swift descent, Otis felt an excruciating pain shoot through his hands. Streams of blood erupted from his freshly sliced digits, as his severed fingers tumbled to the floor. Swiftly another security guard brandishing a handheld blow torch appeared. With a steady hand and a cold determination, he proceeded to cauterize each of the bleeding wounds. The protests of Otis fell upon deaf ears.

In the family home nestled in the heart of Birmingham, the young girl's spirits were gradually mending from the harrowing experience they had endured. The tell-tale marks of violence were gradually losing their prominence. Three sunsets had come and gone since the monstrous presence of Otis and the men. Jolene had refrained from returning to the party houses, heeding Shady's warning to abstain, until her strength had been fully restored.

However, as the men were away, Jolene found herself inundated with a series of ominous messages. Each one carried with it the chilling news that their establishments had fallen victim to police raids, leaving them no choice but to shut down their operations indefinitely. All though, any evidence remained elusive, leaving the police bereft of any means to substantiate their suspicions.

The tenancy agreements, bore the signatures of various aliases, rendering any connection to the nefarious activities utterly inscrutable. Jolene's heart raced, anxiety coursing through her veins like a potent elixir. The absence of any messages from Shady worried her, leaving a bitter taste in her mouth. The silence was deafening. Not a single call from Otis had graced the walls of the house either. She discreetly contacted her circle of trusted friends, desperately seeking refuge for herself and Alice.

The chilling reality revealed itself as each friend, gripped by fear, shied away from the perilous proposition. Jolene had reached a resolute conclusion. The only conceivable path to freedom lay in a daring escape across the Irish sea. The night ferries had a reputation for easy crossings. Passport control, a mere formality, was often overlooked, allowing individuals to slip through undetected.

This was but a fleeting idea, one of many plans. Undeterred, she remained resolute in her determination to secure a means of escape for herself and Alice. Jolene's mind was consumed by the looming threat of Otis's impending return. As she pondered the possibilities, a chilling thought gripped her soul - would Otis, in his insidious machinations, force her and Alice to work the perilous streets.

Her mind was full of uncertainty, torn between two treacherous paths. The once secure confines of their home had been tainted, rendered inhospitable by an unseen menace. Perhaps, just perhaps, the unforgiving streets held a glimmer of relief, a faint promise of sanctuary amidst the chaos. Maria had always preferred to be there, maybe they would also grow accustomed to being there. What was she thinking? the only option was to escape.

CHAPTER 32: Bloodied and battered.

In the confines of the seedy hotel room, Otis and Shady found themselves imprisoned, their fates hanging in the balance. The air was claustrophobic, as the weight of their predicament bore down upon them. Bloodied and battered, their bodies bore the scars of a violent encounter. However, the Palmers woman had extended a helping hand.

With her connections and resources, she arranged for a doctor to tend to their wounds, a gesture of goodwill that could not be ignored. In their world such acts of kindness were a rarity. Shady knew she had sent the doctor, because he had to take a beating too, else Otis would have surely killed him. Otis found himself slipping in and out of consciousness, his mind veering in and out of delirium.

The once innocuous wounds that marred his body had now become a breeding ground for infection. Shady had received word of the impending closure of the houses. His blood boiled with an infernal rage, scorching his veins as he cursed his own weakness for succumbing to Otis's dominance. The flames of fury licked at his conscience, searing his pride and leaving behind only the bitter taste of regret.

How could he have allowed himself to be manipulated by Otis. The echoes of his own cowardice reverberated through his mind, haunting him. In Otis's relentless pursuit of power, he had squandered almost everything they had worked for. The Palmers, once loyal allies, now shunned him with disdain, leaving him bereft of any hope for future profits from their lucrative shipments. Even the young girls who once toiled under their employ, possessed the wisdom to flee from the clutches of Otis. Shady, finally had time to himself to think clearly now that Otis was unconscious once more.

His sister, Sherry, had become distant, evading his every attempt to uncover the truth. Mrs. Palmer had proven to be an invaluable source of information, her revelations granting Shady an unprecedented level of insight. Otis had been throwing his weight around far beyond the confines of his own domain. Not content with merely assaulting his own girls, he possessed a twisted mind that led him to target the innocent girls that worked for the Palmers as well.

The Palmers were notorious for their extravagant parties, where the presence of underage girls were strictly forbidden. Instead, they indulged in a more sophisticated and risqué affair, hosting their gatherings at exclusive venues that catered to the elite. These soirées were graced by the company of high-class call girls, mature women who possessed an air of mystery and allure. Mar, a woman of sophistication, had adamantly rejected the boys plans to follow in Otis's footsteps.

Her piercing gaze cutting through their feeble attempts. With a voice as sharp as a blade, she delivered a stern admonishment to her sons, her disappointment laid bare upon their misguided minds, for even daring to entertain such treacherous schemes. Her face contorted with a mixture of disdain and repulsion as she looked at her boys. The ones who had foolishly granted Otis entry into their world, were swiftly stripped of their esteemed positions, their status within the ranks plummeting like a stone. But that was not all, they were not to escape unscathed. A reckoning was in order, a punishment befitting their transgressions. They were subjected to a thorough beating, a painful reminder of the consequences that awaited those who dared to betray her trust. Mrs. Palmer divulged to Shady every sordid detail of the suspicious murders, the folder brimming with incriminating evidence, and every nefarious act that Otis had ever committed, as if a torrent of darkness was pouring forth from her lips.

The old woman, with her weathered face and piercing gaze, held court as she delved into the depths of Otis's nefarious deeds. With each passing moment, Shady found himself inexplicably drawn to the tales that spilled from the woman's lips. It was as if a bond had formed between the two. She had extended an enticing proposition to Shady, a proposition that would intertwine their fates in the most unexpected of ways. A job, she had proposed, a position as her trusted driver. She had discerned something peculiar about him, an unwavering loyalty that resonated deep within his being. It was this very quality that had captivated her, drawing her towards him like a moth to a flame. Shady emerged from the Palmers club, a different man. As he stepped out into the cold, unforgiving air, clutching Otis tightly in his arms, a realisation washed over him like a tidal wave. Enough was enough. Determination etched across his face, he made a solemn vow to himself - he would do whatever it took to protect the girls. And then, without hesitation, he would vanish into the night, returning to the distant shores of Trinidad, where his mother and sister awaited his safe return.

CHAPTER 33: Mercy.

Five long, agonising days passed before Otis began to mend his broken body. Throughout this arduous period, Shady, remained steadfastly at his side, tending to his wounds with care. With a steady hand, he soothed Otis, his touch gentle yet firm. Fury consumed Otis as he surveyed his bandaged hands, a brutal encounter with the Palmers' ruthless henchmen. His body bore the scars of their merciless blades, a stark reminder to the violence that had unfolded. His flesh was savagely lacerated, the blade leaving a trail of open wounds across his body. No mercy was shown, as the assailants left their mark on him, even desecrating his very manhood.

Shady quietly wished they had chopped it off completely, for it would have undoubtedly spared a multitude of innocent souls from a grim fate. Shady's once tender sentiments towards Otis had withered away, leaving behind a bitter residue of disdain. In his eyes, Otis had transformed into a grotesque creature, no different from his wretched mother, who undoubtedly met her fiery demise in the depths of hell, paying for her heinous transgressions.

Otis slumped in defeat, his shoulders hunched and his gaze downcast. Shady, however, saw through the facade, recognising the calculated ploy. Deep within the recesses of his heart, Shady knew that Otis, with his penchant for playing the victim, skillfully manipulated those in his inner circle, effortlessly winning their sympathy and loyalty. Upon discovering Otis's heinous act of extinguishing the innocent life of young Lorna, an overwhelming desire consumed him - to maintain a considerable distance from Otis, but he was not willing to return to his homeland devoid of spoils. He concocted a scheme, a daring plot to pilfer the contents of Otis's impregnable safe, ensconced within the confines of his offices. Within it lay a treasure trove of illicit delights - a sizable package of cocaine, its white powder street value worth unknown. And nestled beside it, a small fortune in cold, hard cash - a staggering sum of sixty thousand pounds. Shady, with a heavy heart, beseeched the heavens for divine intervention, wishing to orchestrate the girls' liberation before embarking the plane to Trinidad. Uncertainty enveloped his mind, leaving him perplexed as to what strategies he could contrive to secure their freedom.

Jolene and Alice, two lost souls, found themselves stuck within the walls of their desolate home for a gruelling five days. The silence that enveloped the house had rendered them perpetually on edge, their senses heightened to the point where even the slightest sound sent them into panic mode. Shady, had at long last reached out to them, though he was cryptic with the details.

As the dust settled and the wounds began to heal, a glimmer of normality had replaced terror. Fate had other plans. Otis's return was imminent, allowing the darkness to hover over their fragile existence. Tomorrow evening, the air would be tainted with his presence once again.

Once more, the fabric of their existence would be torn apart, the two young girls were still haunted by the harrowing experience they had endured. Their only comforting thoughts lay in the fragile hope that Otis had suffered such grievous injuries, rendering him temporarily incapacitated and granting them a fleeting respite from his tormenting and unrelenting actions.

Shady maintained his silence during the journey back to Birmingham, his mind consumed with plotting his next steps. The venomous words that escaped Otis's lips were like poisonous darts, but Shady refused to let them penetrate his resolve. Otis's voice echoed through the tiny confines of the car, a cacophony of madness and desperation. His words spilled forth like a torrent, each syllable laced with a deranged fervour. The air crackled with the intensity of his rant, as if his very presence had unleashed a storm of chaos. His eyes, once filled with a glimmer of humanity in his youth, now gleamed with a cold, calculating malice. "That Palmer woman who has stripped me of everything." His eyes narrowed as he uttered the words through gritted teeth. "The audacity of the old crone, daring to instruct me on matters of conduct.

Who does she think she is." He vowed to exact a heavy toll for her transgressions. He eagerly anticipated the moment when he would slice through her skin. He vowed to inflict upon her a torment so profound, so excruciating, that its echoes would reverberate through the chambers of time. "She, along with her boys. Every one of them shall tremble before my feet. By the time my wrath has been unleashed, they shall wish our paths had never crossed." Foaming at the mouth, his words sliced through the stifling atmosphere.' The girls will be lucrative assets. I will sell them to the highest bidders. How dare Jolene thing she can outwit me. The business will flourish once again. I will build back better, under my command. They owe me."

Shady's keen ears intercepted the final fragments of Otis's venomous diatribes, yet he remained tight-lipped, refusing to provide Otis with any leverage. Otis, with a flicker of suspicion in his eyes, observed Shady intently. If Otis truly believed that Shady was an ally, he wouldn't be scrutinising him with such intensity. Little did Otis know, Shady, was quietly plotting to undermine him. With a sense of urgency, he resolved to inform the Palmers of Otis's sinister machinations and his current whereabouts. He harboured no doubt that Otis's menacing words would not sit well within the esteemed walls of the Palmer Firm. Otis embodied the ferocity of a rabid canine, his relentless pursuit akin to a beast unleashed. Otis had narrowly evaded the clutches of death, but he was too egotistical to see reality. The man he had once held dear, a bond akin to that of brothers, appeared utterly ignorant. He truly believed himself to be invincible.

The journey home stretched out before Shady like an endless ribbon of asphalt, winding through the darkened countryside. The night air was heavy, broken only by the low hum of his engine. Every passing mile seemed to deepen the sense of unease that clung to him like a second skin. Otis continued his frenzied tirade without pause, his words spilling forth like a torrential downpour.

Needing breaks, Shady found himself drawn to the service stations that lined the route leading him back home. These havens offered him a temporary reprieve from the burdens that weighed heavily upon his weary mind. Otis made a decision to remain concealed within the confines of the car during their frequent stops. His instincts, honed by years of evading the watchful eyes of law enforcement, warned him against attracting any unnecessary attention. The bandages wrapped tightly around his hands, concealing the wounds inflicted upon him.

Though, they could not contain the steady trickle of fluid that oozed through, staining the fabric, and creating a grotesque spectacle. Shady swiftly dialled the number, his voice low and urgent as he warned the girls of Otis's darkening mood. Jolene was tasked with retrieving her mother's sleeping tablets. Their plan was simple, once Otis returned home, they would surreptitiously slip one of those potent pills into his unsuspecting drink. Granting them some breathing space from Otis. Shady, made a solemn promise to Jolene. He vowed to remain within their house for a few days, concealing his true desires beneath a facade of compliance. Little did she know, this was the last thing he wanted. His sole desire was to shield the innocent girls from harm, their desperate need for his presence outweighed his own needs.

Jolene's fingers trembled as she replaced the receiver, her teeth sinking into her lower lip. "Alice," she whispered urgently, her voice laced with desperation, "We need to find mothers stash." In a flurry of desperation, Alice dashed up the staircase, her heart pounding in her chest. Her destination, the airing cupboard. With a swift motion, she retrieved her mother's medicine tub. With a sense of urgency, she descended the staircase, clutching the item tightly in her hand.

Her pace quickened as she approached Jolene. Alice's lips curled into a mischievous grin, her eyes glinting with a devious spark. "Why don't we crush a handful of these," she suggested, her voice a mere whisper, yet resolute. "Alice," Jolene whispered. "I could kiss you." With a sly smile, she produced four sleeping tablets, their presence concealed within the palm of her hand. Placing them delicately on a plate resting upon the table, she proceeded to crush them with precision. Jolene's face lit up with a sinister smile, "We can add some of Otis's rum and dissolve it in Otis's treasured tankard." Their eyes gleamed with a triumphant glint, their gazes fixated on the dissolving tablets.

"This will work I'm sure of it". Said Alice with a jubilant smile.

Jolene and Alice found themselves captivated by Shady's every word. The mere thought of liberation seemed too audacious to fathom, hope began to ignite within them. Their sole preoccupation revolved around the unsettling revelation that Shady had declared his imminent departure, leaving them in the dubious care of Otis for a span of one or two weeks.

During this time, Shady intended to reconnect with his acquaintances and kin, in a desperate bid to secure their assistance. He insisted on making a personal appearance, fully aware of the gravity of the situation. Shady, told the girls he had a nest egg, which he would use part of it to reward anyone willing to help them. His mind raced, contemplating the possibilities that lay before him. Jolene's voice trembled with genuine fear as she inquired about his welfare. With a determined glint in his eyes, he told her of his plans. " There's no need to fret over my well-being, once your settled I will go back to my roots, Trinidad." They all nodded in agreement, sealing their fate.

The remainder of their evening consisted of board games, which Sherry had bought for their amusement. Shady, with a heavy heart, concealed the truth about Otis's sinister intentions from the girls. He deemed it wiser to grant the young girls a mere glimmer of hope, rather than burdening them with the weight of his sombre revelations. A sense of apprehension was burrowing deep within his gut. Reluctantly, he contemplated the prospect of leaving them to Otis's care. It was a decision he dreaded.

Although circumstances left him with no other choice. He felt it was his duty to ensure a secure future for the young girls before his imminent departure from the country. The weight of this responsibility pressed upon him. The path ahead was fraught with danger, but he remained undeterred, his every step guided by a sense of purpose. Shady had a devious plan in mind as he contemplated how to approach Otis.

It was a tale of sorrow and loss, a story of a funeral that never took place. Shady intended to convince Otis that it was his own mother's sister who had passed away, a tragedy that demanded his immediate attention. But Shady's cunning didn't stop there. He knew that to truly deceive Otis, he had to play the role of the dutiful executor. With a calculated charm, he would inform Otis that he alone held the responsibility of settling the deceased aunt's affairs. It was a ploy to keep Otis from questioning his absence for an extended period of time, under the guise of fulfilling his duties.

CHAPTER 34: Left alone.

The once lively home had transformed into a sombre sanctuary, emotions ran high and seemed to cling to the walls. Otis's devilish figure at the centre of it all, lay motionless in his bed, he had slept for days. The girls had covertly ground the potent sleeping tablets into his beverages, repeating this act on multiple occasions, all to maintain his docility. Shady, ever the astute observer, had caught wind of their scheme and promptly delivered a stern admonition, emphasising the perilous consequences of an overdose. Yet, beneath his disapproval, a begrudging admiration simmered for their resourcefulness. After giving the girls a stern talking to, Shady had to remind them of his imminent trip.

The girls were saddened by Shady's words, frustration etched on their beautiful faces. Deep within their hearts, they harboured the unsettling realisation that their scheming could not carry on indefinitely. Time was also creeping up on them. Shortly Shady would have to leave them, alone with Otis. Shady's presence, was fleeting and could only be guaranteed for a mere two days longer. Then Shady would have to forge onward with his plans to secure their escape. The girls, their eyes gleaming with determination, looked Shady square in the eye.

They exuded an air of confidence, that only hope can bring. They assured him, in hushed tones, that they were prepared to face whatever Otis had planned for them. Their voices, laced with a newfound resolve. They knew, deep down in their souls, that a brighter future awaited them, just beyond the horizon. Jolene's concern for Alice far outweighed any personal anxieties that plagued her.

Alice's heart raced as she fervently whispered her prayers, desperately seeking the strength to confront the sinister plans that Otis had in store for them. Neither of the young girls possessed a clear understanding of Otis's deviant intentions, fear lingered within their hearts. They were acutely aware that he intended to subject them to a harrowing existence, a life of exploitation, where their bodies would be ruthlessly sold for monetary gain. With every fibre of their being, they were consumed by an overwhelming sense of dread.

Jolene had grown accustomed to the despicable reality that plagued her existence, though no innocent child should ever be subjected to such heinous violations of her body. But Alice, was still so young, and had only experienced exploitation on two occasions. One of these encounters, a hazy memory tainted by the influence of drugs. Jolene couldn't shake off the nagging thoughts that consumed her mind. Determined to confront the matter head-on, she resolved to have a discreet conversation with Alice, ensuring that Otis remained oblivious to their discussion.

"MEMORIES"

'Maria confided in me and shared her deepest, darkest secret. What to do when different men want to have sexual encounters with me. She instructed me to shut out the world and focus on something else in my head. Sometimes I'm a famous dancer, dancing as if my life depended on it. Adored and loved by all, and other times I'm riding a horse on a cool summer's breeze, just at the shoreline on a sandy beach. At other times, I simply think about the people I care about and everything they've done to make my life better. Maria told me, "It's how to keep them from devouring your spirit; your heart and spirit belong to you and only you."

Otis descended the staircase, his countenance a tempestuous storm. His head throbbed, leaving him in a state of grogginess and lingering dizziness. The two sisters leaned in, their ruby lips brushing against his cheek in a tender gesture. "Good morning, dad," they chimed in unison. "We hope that you're feeling better." Alice's voice dripped with saccharine sweetness, and with a deceptive charm.

Meanwhile, Jolene, prepared a cup of coffee for him. Shady, dishevelled, and weary from yet another restless night on the sofa, finally joined their ranks. As the group gathered around the table, sipping their steaming cups of coffee, tension soared. Each of them couldn't help but notice the subtle shift in Otis's demeanour, a disquieting transformation that seemed to render him more unhinged than ever before. "Once we've finished our brekkie, it's imperative that we change those bandages," Shady declared.

Otis cast a discerning gaze upon him, his eyes narrowing as he perceived the unmistakable worry etched upon his companion's face. With a measured pause, he finally responded, his voice laced with a hint of weariness, "Very well brother. I am starving." The kitchen exhaled a collective sigh of relief, as if the very walls themselves were grateful for the respite. Harmony was finally reinstated, a tranquil aura fell over the room. They gathered around the table, united by a shared meal, as if the tumultuous events of the past had never transpired. Even Jolene, succumbed to the prevailing atmosphere and cautiously indulged in a morsel of toast, careful not to disturb the delicate balance that had been painstakingly restored.

The sisters made a valiant effort to avert their gaze from Otis's hands, covered in bandages that concealed the gruesome aftermath, of his recent ordeal. Despite their best attempts, the sight of his wounded appendages, still oozing vital fluids where the searing heat had sealed the wounds, proved to be an unsettling spectacle. Otis, bore the unmistakable mark of his troubled past - his hands, forever marred by the absence of his last two fingers. These missing digits, a ghastly indication to a life lived on the edge. The sight before them was nothing short of grotesque. His countenance bore the unmistakable signs of the violence he had endured. On either cheek, the jagged scars told a harrowing tale of a blade's merciless journey through his once unblemished flesh.

"MEMORIES"

'I'm glad they cut his fingers off, and I'm even happier that they scarred his face for life. Maybe now women will run away from him. He is so ugly, now. He now has the appearance of the monstrosity that he is. It was challenging for me to conceal my genuine emotions from him, especially the gratitude I felt towards those who had tortured him. It is no longer possible for him to rely on his good looks to attract ladies into his life. Tomorrow will be Shady's last day here, and I'm terrified of what lies ahead. I had a conversation with Alice and shared the secret that Maria and I had been keeping, which was about how to withdraw within oneself and block off the outside world. She claimed that she performs it on a regular basis, therefore it shouldn't be too difficult for her to do. Thank you, God, for making sure that horrible person got what was coming to him, he earned every cut and every scar.'

CHAPTER 35: The carparks.

Shady gathered his belongings, his mind clouded with a sense of impending doom. With a heavy heart, he pressed his lips against the cheeks of both girls, bidding them farewell. As he strode away, the weight of guilt settled upon his conscience. He knew Otis was consumed by a frenzied madness, the fate of the girls, as of yet was unknown. Shady, held the key to their salvation.

Should Shady fail, the girls would be condemned to a life devoid of any glimmer of hope, forever trapped in their harrowing predicament. As he slid into the sleek leather seat of his car, his gaze lingered on the two young girls, their delicate figures looked so small, in the ominous shadow of Otis's towering presence. Like a malevolent ogre, he loomed over them. In that moment, a profound sorrow gripped his heart, shattering it into a thousand fragmented pieces.

An evil sensation crept over him, whispering that Otis, would not be inclined to show them mercy. Otis found himself in a dire financial bind, his once abundant wealth now reduced to mere ashes. Accustomed to a life of opulence and luxury, it was only natural for him to contemplate a sinister solution to his monetary woes - a decision that would lead him to exploit the vulnerable sisters, forcing them into the streets, where survival was a constant battle.

Jolene and Alice bid him farewell with a sombre wave, their faces etched with weariness and sorrow, their eyes haunted by the shadows of sleepless nights. With a decisive click, Otis shut the door, severing the connection to the outside world. The girls were ordered to clean the kitchen and the chaotic house. Meanwhile, Otis, perched at the kitchen table, immersed himself in deep contemplation, planning his next moves.

With a swift and silent motion, Otis seized his car keys, as if possessed by an urgent purpose. Without a word, he slipped away from the confines of the house, leaving behind a trail of unanswered questions. Not a word escaped his lips as he abandoned the young girls, leaving them in a state of bewildered silence.

Alice fixed her eyes on the empty chair where Otis had once sat. Her voice trembled as she posed her question, her eyes darting nervously around the kitchen." Where did he go?" Jolene answered,

" I hope he stays away". Her lips curved upward, forming a smile that didn't reach her eyes. With fear and loathing, Alice's voice sliced through the air, "I hope he dies. I hope we never have to see him again."

"Me too. Now let's get this house cleaned up, shall we, the last thing we need is Otis to come back to a dirty house."

Jolene berated herself for her abruptness with which she had chosen to conclude their conversation. With a shared determination, the sisters started the arduous chores. Their motivation stemmed not from a desire for cleanliness, but rather from a desperate need to prevent Otis, known for his explosive rages, from finding any reason to unleash his wrath upon them.

Two days had passed, each one dragging on with an unbearable weight, before Otis finally materialised at the doorstep of the home. The moonless night cloaked his arrival, his intentions in an impenetrable darkness. With a thunderous entrance, he burst into the house, his anger palpable in the air.

Without warning, he hurled clothes towards the unsuspecting girls, their startled expressions mirroring their confusion. His voice, filled with an undeniable menace, demanded that they hastily dress themselves in the garments he had acquired for them. He had procured for them denim miniskirts and crop tops. They carried out his every command, oblivious to the dangers that would befall them. In the warmth of the kitchen, Otis's restless footsteps echoed against the floor.

His voice, laced with impatience, reverberated through the air, urging them to hurry up. As the sisters prepared themselves, he commanded them to get their coats, as they were venturing into the coldness of night. Alice and Jolene exchanged a knowing glance, their lips sealed tight, unwilling to stoke the smouldering embers of his wrath. The two girls found themselves in uncomfortable attire, they looked like cheap tarts, and they hated it. Otis had never bought them anything in the past.

The skirts, were extremely short barely covering their knickers, sparking unease within the girls. With a screech of tyres, Otis sped away from the house as if the devil himself was on his tail. In the back seat, the two young girls shivered, their innocent faces etched with fear. As the engine roared, Otis unleashed a torrent of vile commands. "You will do as your told tonight. You owe me and now I'm collecting." His chilling tone cutting through the girls like a sharp razor blade. "You will have sex with various men tonight.

You will make them happy, they have paid me handsomely. You will do whatever they ask of you, or you will suffer the consequences. Do you understand me girls? Now be good girls for daddy and do as your told. If either of you dare to provoke me, the repercussions shall be dire." As Jolene and her sister arrived at the desolate carpark, a threatening sensation washed over her.

Dread settled in her gut, as if sensing the impending danger. This was the moment she had feared, the culmination of her suspicions. While he had been absent, he had been orchestrating this sinister plan. She understood all too well that there existed no alternative but to comply with his commands. Her soul ached for her sister. Alice's eyes widened, fear gripping her like a vice.

She was a pawn in a game she didn't understand. She found herself in a perplexing predicament, unsure of how to proceed. She had never had to satisfy men sexually before, with exception of the instances when she was rendered helpless by drugs or restraints. Six vehicles, their engines silenced, sat motionless in the carpark. Inside each car, a group of men, their faces hidden, anxiously awaited the arrival of the girls. Jolene's fingers wrapped around Alice's hand, a gentle yet firm grip that conveyed unspoken words.

Otis emerged from the sanctuary of his vehicle. With a calculated brutality, he seized the young girls by their delicate arms, wrenching them from the confines of the car. The sheer strength of his grip mirrored the destructive power of a hurricane, leaving no doubt as to the depths of his depravity. He forcefully propelled Alice towards the awaiting vehicle, flinging open the rear door.

Alice's fragile form was callously hurled into the clutches of the leering men who hungered for her body. Her feeble resistance proved futile as she found herself in his overpowering grasp, her senses barely registering the swift turn of events. In the blink of an eye, the door sealed her fate with a resounding slam. A chilling air of malevolence pervaded the space as the men descended upon her, their hands clawing and tearing at her underwear. Smothering her in their foul breath and forcing their tongues in her mouth.

They groped relentlessly at her body, nothing was sacred. Jolene pleaded with Otis, her voice full of desperation, it fell on deaf ears. Jolene's world shattered with a resounding slap, leaving a stinging imprint on her delicate cheek. The forceful blow jolted her senses, awakening a primal fear within. With an iron grip, he seized her trembling form and forcefully propelled her towards another vehicle, lurking like a predator in the night. Jolene made the fateful choice to relinquish her resistance and embrace the inevitable.

The continual passage of time stretched on, as if hours had morphed into an eternity, before the girls were finally granted freedom from their servitude. They were left shaken and petrified. At least there was a small mercy that the perpetrators, had refrained from any brutality upon them. As the night wore on, their lewd remarks echoed through the air. They shamelessly indulged in the girls' vulnerability, their bodies mere objects to be possessed. Alice found herself immersed in the darkness her sister had tried to shield her from.

On this fateful evening, words whispered into her ears that she had never encountered. Meanwhile, a burning sensation ignited between her thighs, consuming her like an inferno. The pain in her legs was a constant reminder of the contorted positions she had been subjected to within the cramped confines of the vehicle. The fleet of cars idled, their engines purring like predatory beasts.

Each vehicle harboured a minimum of four predatory males, all eager to rape the young girls. All taking turns to have their wicked way with them. They didn't seem to care that the girls were underage, all they were interested in, was taking, what was not theirs to take. They wanted the girl's bodies to fulfil their own perverted desires. The girls screams and cries only heightened their excitement, Alice had quickly realised this, and reverted into herself, refusing to even let a whimper escape her lips as they pounded her body.

The night had reached its conclusion finally, and Otis was taking them home. Not a word had left Otis's lips throughout their entire journey. Meanwhile, in the backseat, Alice and Jolene clung to each other, their delicate hands intertwined as tears streamed down their flawless features.

CHAPTER 36: Unspeakable.

Otis manoeuvred his vehicle with calculated precision, bringing it to a halt just outside the house. With an air of authority, he barked at the young girls, his voice laced with an unmistakable menace, compelling them to make their way indoors.

The girls breathed a collective sigh of relief as they discovered that Otis had chosen to remain in the car. With cautious steps, they approached their front door, their bones weary. As the engine roared to life, and with a screech of tyres, he vanished into the night, leaving the girls home alone. Jolene ascended the staircase with a determined stride, her body aching with every step.

Ignoring the protests of her weary muscles, she hastened to prepare a bath for the two of them. Alice trailed behind her, her eyes fixated on her sister. They shed their garments, revealing the vulnerability of their persecuted souls. As the steamy tendrils of the water enveloped them, they both were lost, in their own silent worlds. Words, once flowing freely between them, now lay splintered and broken, casualties of the unspeakable horrors they had been through.

The weight of their shared trauma suffocating any semblance of conversation. They still hadn't heard from Shady, had he forgotten about them? Would there be salvation or abandonment. Would he prove faithful, or had he forsaken them in their hour of need?

Only time would reveal the truth, as they clung to a fragile thread of optimism, praying that Shady had not vanished, leaving them to face their fate alone. In the bedroom, there was only the sound of their breathing. Jolene's heart pounded in her chest, each beat a reminder of the perilous situation they found themselves in. She closed her eyes, as her mind focused on Shady, the one they had placed their hopes upon.

Prayers whispered into the heavens, neither of the girls knew how much more they could endure. How long before their bodies and minds and souls would be broken. Weariness consumed their bodies, rendering them powerless to resist. Their eyes, heavy with fatigue, could no longer withstand the weight of wakefulness. In a silent accord, devoid of verbal exchange, they succumbed to the embrace of slumber, whilst holding on to each other for dear life.

EACH PASSING DAY, OTIS would retreat, leaving them to their own devices, only to resurface at night-time, imposing upon them the relentless torment that had become their grim routine. In the various car parks, a series of men would await them. Though the locations differed, the chilling outcome remained unchanged, their bodies violated, their innocence stolen.

Alice, once a spirited girl, now found herself imprisoned by the confines of her own mind. Selective mutism had become her constant companion, rendering her voiceless in a world that desperately needed her words. The once vibrant conversations that filled the air had now become a distant memory, replaced by a haunting silence that echoed through the corridors of her existence. On rare occasions her response would be succinct, a single word only and never in front of Otis. Their frail forms concealed the damning evidence they had been subjected to.

"MEMORIES"

'I wish Alice would talk to me, she barely says a word these days. We are both lost in our own misery. Every night it's the same, a different car park, different men. But it's the same endless nightmare. There's still no sign of Shady, has he forgotten us? It's nearly been three weeks, three weeks of torture. I'm losing hope. Will we ever get away from Otis? I'm beginning to think myself and Alice should just leave, but then I worry that Otis has someone watching us, making sure we don't leave the house during the day. If we were to run, I think we would have to do it at night after the carparks, when Otis drops us back home. I don't think Alice can handle much more, she is a shadow of her former self".

As the veil of night descended, casting an eerie ambiance upon the unsuspecting victims. Otis made an appearance once again. With a voice as sharp as a blade, he barked orders at the sisters, compelling them to prepare themselves hastily, for time was of the essence.

Alice's body was aching, her spirit dampened by a relentless illness that had plagued her throughout the day. Yet, Otis, with his cold indifference, remained unfazed by her suffering. His commands were delivered with a cold, unyielding tone, leaving no room for negotiation.

His words, piercing through the silence of the room. It was a demand that brooked no resistance, "You will work tonight, whether you are ill or not. The necessary arrangements had been made". The words echoed through the home, the air thick with tension. His voice, low and menacing, cut through the silence like a knife. "I cannot let you stay at home," he growled, his eyes narrowing with a dangerous glint.

She felt a shiver crawl up her spine, her heart pounding in her chest. The room seemed to close in around her. His piercing gaze bore into the two sisters, his eyes ablaze with menace. Jolene's feeble protest escaped her lips, "but dad," she pleaded, her eyes darting anxiously, "she is truly unwell. What if, she pukes in the cars or on those men?" In that very moment, Alice's stomach revolted, unleashing a torrent of vomit that splattered across the pristine surfaces of the kitchen.

Tremors coursed through Alice's frame, a visceral reaction to the eruption of violence that had unfolded within her. In that moment, Otis's eyes widened with a sudden realisation, of Alice's affliction. Jolene found herself at the mercy of a perilous predicament. The man before her, seething with fury, declared that the burden of servicing the men would fall solely upon her shoulders this evening.

It was a decision made out of necessity, for Alice was in a wretched state, her body drenched in her own vomit. With a stern gaze, he demanded, "Clean up this wretched mess, and then clean yourself up," his finger pointing accusingly at Alice. "We are late, let's go," he ordered. In a swift and forceful motion, Otis seized Jolene's arm, his grip tight and unyielding.

With a menacing resolve, he propelled her out of the confines of the house, thrusting her into the biting embrace of the frigid night air. Without a moment's hesitation, he flung her into the waiting vehicle. Alone in the desolate house, Alice's frailty consumed her, rendering her as feeble as a defenceless kitten. Yet, she understood the grim necessity of her task - to rid the repugnant stench of vomit that permeated the air. She procured a bucket for her own sickness, alongside a bowl brimming with scalding water. Tears streamed down her face, mingling with the filth, as she commenced the arduous process of cleansing the tainted kitchen.

CHAPTER 37: Frozen.

Three long and treacherous weeks had elapsed since Shady's sudden departure, leaving them in a state of perpetual unease. As the sun began its descent, casting an ominous shadow over the horizon, the girls braced themselves for the inevitable. They were all too aware of the impending danger, Otis's sinister presence that had become all too familiar.

The days blended together seamlessly, like a never-ending reel of their tortured existence. Every night he would fling garments towards them, garments that were scandalously short and tantalisingly low-cut. A commanding voice would pierce the silence, compelling them to obediently follow his lead, as they journeyed through the maze of carparks scattered across the urban landscape.

Tonight, the air was humid and dense, as if a storm was brewing on the horizon. Jolene couldn't help but notice the peculiar glint in Alice's eyes. It was a look of a startled deer, her eyes were glazed. Something had shaken Alice to her core, she was getting more distant lately, and seemed to revert within her being, as if hiding from the real world. Jolene's attempts at engaging in conversation with her proved futile, for it seemed as though she had become as responsive as the impassive walls that surrounded them.

Jolene's voice quivered, "Alice, please speak to me." Alice's gaze pierced through her, a chilling intensity. It was as if she had become a prisoner of her own mind, trapped within the corridors of her thoughts. No external force could wrench her away from the intricate world she had spun within her own consciousness. Jolene gently approached, her intentions full of compassion.

Alice, lost in her own world of torment, recoiled instinctively, oblivious to the fact that it was Jolene. Jolene's hands were reaching out, as she pleaded with Alice, her voice laced with anguish. "Please, Alice, snap out of it," she implored, her heart pounding in her chest.

"You're worrying me, sis. I need you. Please, come back to me." "Speak to me," she pleaded, the silence broken only by the faint sound of her racing heartbeat. Jolene's flawless bone structure was marred by the rivulets of frustration that cascaded down her delicate features. Alice's countenance mirrored that of a startled deer caught in the blinding glare of headlights.

Her once rosy complexion had drained away, leaving behind a ghostly pallor. The intensity in her eyes betrayed a tumultuous storm brewing within her. And then, as if retreating into the depths of her own thoughts, she finally found her voice. "I'm so sorry," she whispered, her words hanging in the air like a fragile thread. "I love you."

Jolene's trembling ceased, her hands steadying as she pulled her sister close, clutching her as if their very survival hinged on this embrace. "Thank the heavens, sis," she whispered, "You must be strong, it won't be long now, I'm sure of it." Jolene's heart shattered as she voiced her deepest fears, her vulnerability laid bare. "Shady will be back soon.

Please stay with me," She begged. Alice was haunted by the harrowing nocturnal excursions to the carpark, even upon returning home. Even when she slept, she would be in a relentless torment, reliving the frightening encounters with her assailants. Each night, the demons of her past would seize her subconscious, etching every detail of those predators into her memory with chilling precision.

With each caress, their perspiring forms became entangled, their fervour unyielding as they took what they wanted from her, night after night, gradually extinguishing fragments of her very soul. Every evening, she found herself trapped in a harrowing routine, forced to endure the unspeakable horrors that unfolded within the car parks. Each night, her spirit shattered as she became a victim of relentless assaults, her very existence tainted by the cruel hands of her tormentors.

But the torment did not cease when she was within the confines of her own home. No, the demons that haunted her followed, invading the sanctuary of her bed, perpetuating the vicious cycle of violation within the realm of her dreams. The weight of her burden proved unbearable, dragging her down into the abyss of desolation. With each passing day, she discovered herself sinking deeper into the abyss of her own mind, struggling to resurface into reality.

The haunting memories like relentless spectres, would seize her whenever she dared to shut her eyes, forcing her to relive the harrowing ordeal that had forever altered her existence. No matter how many baths she indulged in, the stains of the past refused to be washed away. She found herself trapped in the clutches of an inescapable nightmare.

Otis manoeuvred the vehicle through the streets of the city, his grip on the steering wheel firm and unyielding. In the backseat, Jolene and Alice clung to each other, their hands intertwined with a desperate intensity. As Jolene and her sister were coerced into the vehicle by the menacing Otis, apprehension enveloped them. Jolene's gaze fixated upon her sister, she was so distant now, and it scared her. Would she ever hear her laugh again?

When they were forced out of the car, Alice appeared to be muttering words under her breath to her sister. Though the words eluded her, it sent an icy tremor coursing through Jolene's veins. Out on the top floor of the car park a fierce struggle ensued, between Otis and Alice. Her eyes ablaze with disobedience, she fought back with every ounce of strength she possessed.

With a flurry of furious strikes, she tore into Otis, her blows landing with a resounding impact. Despite the odds stacked against her, Alice was relentless. In a desperate attempt to gain the upper hand, she aimed her kicks at Otis's vulnerable groin, her petite legs flailing in the air. Each attempt, though valiant, narrowly missed its intended target, leaving Alice frustrated but undeterred.

The car park echoed with the sounds of their fierce clash, a symphony of grunts and gasps, as the battle raged on. Jolene's desperate pleas echoed through the air as Alice unleashed her fury, their struggle intensifying. "Please, Alice," Jolene's voice begged, her words dripped with fear. "Stop this madness, please." The air was thick with the weight of her futile cries. No matter how fervently she begged, her pleas were but whispers in the wind. With a surge of adrenaline coursing through her veins, Alice summoned every ounce of strength within her.

In a swift, calculated motion, she delivered a resounding blow to Otis's most vulnerable region - his groin. The excruciating pain seized him, causing his grip on Alice to loosen, granting her the freedom she so desperately sought. Alice bolted through the parked cars, her heart pounding like a drum in her chest. Every fibre of her being screamed at her to flee, as if the very essence, of evil was hot on her heels.

Meanwhile, Otis, his pain momentarily forgotten, mustered every ounce of strength he had to carry out his pursuit. Determination etched across his face, he raced after Alice, his legs propelling him forward with unwavering resolve. As the chase unfolded, a sinister quartet emerged from the confines of their vehicle. With ages spanning from the prime of their twenties to the twilight of their thirties, these men joined the pursuit, their predatory instincts awakened, closing in on her with each passing moment.

Otis grimaced as he fought against the pain radiating from his once-injured leg, each step a reminder of the car accident that had left him hobbled. Determined to catch her, he pushed through the hindrance, his speed compromised but in firm resolve. Jolene's blood-curdling scream pierced the air. The events unfolded with a swiftness that defied comprehension, leaving her paralysed with fear.

She stood frozen, her heart pounding in her chest as she bore witness to the disintegration of her very existence. In the midst of Alice's desperate bid for freedom from her tormentors, a sudden and unexpected figure Otis, materialised out of thin air. With an unfathomable strength, he propelled himself towards Alice. The sheer magnitude of his assault sent shockwaves through her fragile frame, causing her to emit a piercing cry that reverberated through the night. In a cruel twist of fate, Alice was propelled over the towering carpark wall, hurtling towards certain death, five floors below.

The world held its breath, awaiting the outcome of this perilous plunge. Jolene's heart raced as she sprinted towards the wall, her eyes fixated on her sister's lifeless form. Alice lay sprawled on the ground, her body contorted in an unnatural manner. A chilling sight greeted Jolene's horrified gaze - a crimson pool of blood oozing from her sister's shattered skull. There was no mistaking it; Alice was gone, forever lost to the clutches of death. Jolene's piercing scream reverberated through the air. Otis had snuffed out her sister's existence, leaving behind a trail of shattered dreams and broken hearts. She had lost her sister. She had been murdered. The truth, as painful as it was, could no longer be denied - Otis was a cold-blooded killer.

CHAPTER 38: The price of freedom.

In a frenzied panic, the men sprinted towards the sanctuary of their vehicles, desperate to flee the grisly tableau of murder that unfolded before them. With a cacophony of screeching tyres, they ignited their engines and sped away, leaving behind a cloud of smoke and a trail of uncertainty.

As Jolene stood there, her heart heavy with the weight of the unspeakable events that had just unfolded, she crumpled in a ball to the floor. Snot, trickled down Jolene's quivering nose, staining her face with a mixture of tears and despair. In the desolate carpark, Jolene's shattered spirit coiled into the foetal position, her body curled up tightly as if seeking refuge from the horrors that she had seen.

Her desperate pleas echoed through the night, trembling with fear and vulnerability. "Please don't leave me," she whispered over and over. The weight of her plea hung heavy, as if the very fabric of her existence depended on those words being heard. Her soul was teetering on the edge of despair.

The raw emotion etched upon her face, her words remained her only defences, her last hope in a world that seemed intent on destroying her. Otis seized her by the luscious strands of her hair, yanking her body upwards. Jolene found herself succumbing to the icy grip of shock, her feeble resistance rendered futile against the strength of Otis. With a sudden burst of rage, he struck her across the cheek, the sound echoing through the desolate night. Undeterred by her pain, he forcefully pulled her towards his vehicle, his countenance mirroring the turbulent skies that mirrored his inner turmoil.

His fury was a tangible force, emanating from him like a dark cloud. He seethed with a venomous rage, his lips spewing forth a torrent of savage words, each one viler than the last. It was as if his very soul had been tainted, and his every utterance dripped with the putrid stench of decay.

With a forceful shove, he propelled her into the recesses of the back seat. Her tears, like tiny rivulets of despair, cascaded down her cheeks, lost in the darkness that enveloped her. Meanwhile, he wasted no time, his movements swift and purposeful, as he assumed his position behind the wheel. Without a moment's hesitation, he unleashed the full power of the engine, propelling them away from the scene of Alice's murder, with a velocity that matched the pounding of their hearts.

As the vintage Mercedes glided to a halt in front of the warmth of the house, Otis cast a steely gaze at Jolene. With a commanding tone, he commanded her to exit the vehicle, his voice dripping with an icy warning that sent shivers down her spine. Keep that trap of yours sealed tight, or you'll find yourself 'DEAD YARN' just like the others. I will murder you, do you understand?" Jolene raced towards the house, her heart pounding in her chest, desperate to escape his clutches.

In this moment, her sole salvation lay in putting as much distance between them as possible. Otis's eyes fixated on Jolene as she firmly shut the front door, her silhouette disappearing into the darkness. With a sudden surge of adrenaline, he stomped on the accelerator, causing his tyres to screech in protest. The acrid scent of burning rubber filled the air, mingling with the thick cloud of smoke that billowed behind him, obscuring his hasty departure.

Jolene, consumed by a torrent of emotions, succumbed to their overwhelming force. In the kitchen, she crumbled, her body giving way to the weight of her sorrow. Seeking some warmth, she clung to herself, swaying back and forth in a desperate attempt to find comfort.

The echoes of her anguished cries bouncing of the walls, as if they bore witness to her torment. In her suffocating despair, she remained oblivious to everything else. The creaking hinges of the front door, as it swung open with calculated silence, went unnoticed by her ears, consumed as they were, by the deafening symphony of her desolation.

Shady stepped into the darkness of the kitchen, his eyes widening in disbelief as he took in the scene before him. With a heavy heart, he lowered himself to the cold, unforgiving floor, his presence causing Jolene to recoil instinctively. The weight of his muscular arms enveloped her petite frame, a stark contrast between his imposing figure and her fragile vulnerability.

He sat there, his presence commanding attention. "I'm back now, what on earth is going on?" his voice heavy with genuine concern. She uttered the name with a tremor in her voice, barely audible. "Alice," she mumbled. The room fell into an eerie silence, the stillness broken only by the sound of her hushed confession. "He has just killed Alice," she whispered.

Her words sliced through him like a sharpened blade, leaving behind a trail of anguish and regret. The realisation dawned upon him, he had arrived too late to rescue them from their torment. The weight of his guilt settled on his shoulders, an oppressive burden that threatened to consume him whole. As Jolene unravelled the sinister tale of their suffering during his absence, the truth became a haunting spectre that refused to be ignored." Listen," he whispered urgently, his voice laced with a sense of impending danger. "We have to make our escape, this wretched place holds nothing but treachery and death.

Time is of the essence. Pack your belongings, we must leave now before Otis returns". With a weary sigh, Jolene finally emerged from her despair, weariness etched upon her face. "It took me longer than I expected," Shady confessed, his voice ladened with regret. "We need to leave tonight." She couldn't ignore the palpable sense of importance that resonated from his every syllable.

Jolene and Shady ascended the staircase with haste, their footsteps echoing through the hallway. Jolene's heart pounded in her chest, her mind racing with thoughts of escape. In the bedroom, Jolene swiftly moved about, her hands trembling as she gathered her belongings. She carefully selected a few articles of clothing, her fingers brushing against the soft fabric as she folded them with precision.

Amongst the garments, she discreetly tucked away one of Alice's nightdresses, a small memento of a life left behind. Jolene then turned her attention to the floorboards. With a deft hand, she pried open the hidden compartment, revealing a stash of money concealed within. Silently, they completed their task, with a sense of urgency. Shady assisted her in hastily gathering her belongings.

As he reached the front room, his eyes fell upon a family portrait resting upon the mantlepiece. In one swift motion, he snatched it from its perch, a memento of happier times, now destined to be a relic of the past. Jolene's tear-stained face bore witness to the anguish that seemed to consume her very soul. The salty droplets cascaded down her cheeks, an unrelenting torrent that refused to abate. Yet, with every fibre of her being, Jolene was determined to escape the clutches of Otis, and the wretched existence that had ensnared her. She yearned to flee, to put as much distance as possible between herself and the life that had become a living nightmare.

As the duo approached Shady's sleek black BMW, his voice pierced through the tension, injecting a glimmer of hope into her weary heart. "Are you ready for your new life? We are heading to Scotland, it's a long trip but I doubt he will find you there". With a roar of the engine, they drove away. Jolene glanced over her shoulder one last time at the house that once held so many memories for her, now it was just a reminder of what she had lost. With every passing mile a glimmer of hope arose within her. She was really free, finally free.

To be continued.

ABOUT THE AUTHOR.
ROXY RICH

I am an author with a disability who lives in Somerset with my two children and husband. My unusual experience, which includes having worked in the sex industry over 17 years ago, serves as a source of inspiration for my writing. It is my duty to bring light on the tales of working girls, the social injustices they suffer. This experience has provided me with unique insights into the life of working girls. I am currently working on my second novel, as I intend to write a whole series that will be devoted to investigating the lives of women who work in the sex industry. Each new installment will focus on a different aspect of their life, thereby delivering a holistic and compassionate perspective of the world in which they live. By combining my years of lived experience with a more mature view on the complexities of the human condition, I believe that now is the ideal time in my life to offer these stories to a broader audience.

Don't miss out!

Click the button below and you can sign up to receive emails whenever Roxy Rich publishes a new book. There's no charge and no obligation.

https://books2read.com/r/B-A-URRMB-ECALD

BOOKS 2 READ

Connecting independent readers to independent writers.